*We have to inspire the next generation. They have
to understand that they can make a difference.*
—Ruby Bridges, Civil Rights icon

the power
OF CHILDREN

**Ordinary Youth
Making Extraordinary
Differences**

CHILDREN'S MUSEUM
INDIANAPOLIS

with Skip Berry and Andrew Kimmel

AuthorHouse™
1663 Liberty Drive
Bloomington, IN 47403
www.authorhouse.com
Phone: 1 (800) 839-8640

Published by AuthorHouse 11/05/2015

ISBN: 978-1-4969-2150-5 (sc)

Library of Congress Control Number: 2015917212

Photo credits:
Kendra Springs photo
Jenni Nattam Photography

Dale Pedzinski photo
Chris Parypa

Christopher Yao
Kids Change The World

IsaacMcFarland
Alliance for a Healthier Generation

Charles Orgbon III
Tangee Renee Photography

Print information available on the last page.

Any people depicted in stock imagery provided by Thinkstock are models,
and such images are being used for illustrative purposes only.
Certain stock imagery © Thinkstock.

This book is printed on acid-free paper.

authorHOUSE®

THE POWER OF CHILDREN

Some become sisters or brothers
Some become aunts, uncles or "in's"
Some become mothers, fathers, grands or even greats
But all are, at once, forever and always, someone's child
We are all, at once, forever and always, children…

The power of children is seen in the young child's sheer joy and glee expressed
In the love they give to those who care, nurture and patiently guide…
In a love of learning
And love of the natural world…

The power of children grows within as we learn to care for others
Our family, our friends and those who came before
For those with less, those with more, those who need our care
The power of children is the power within to care for and nurture all

The power of children is the power to live our lives as nurturing, caring adults

To ensure that all children, everywhere, are loved, are healthy and
learn to care for and nurture others throughout their lives

Those who use this power remain, forever and always,
true and eternal children of the world

The power of children is the power to transform the world.

—Jeffrey Patchen, 2011

Thanks to the Deborah Joy Simon Charitable Trust for making this all possible.

The Power of Children Awards celebrate young people who help to make the world a better place. Over the past 10 years, 50 winners have made an enormous impact. **How will you change the world?**

10 Years of Impact

Launched in Indiana, grown nationwide

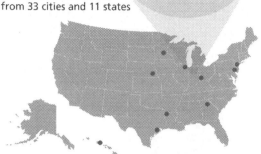

50 winners
from 33 cities and 11 states

20,074 hours
of winners' personal time commitments

Over $10 million
raised by winners for projects

Touched 57 countries

1,719,685 people directly benefited

800,000 +
people fed

555,000 +
children benefited

100,000 +
soldiers supported

5,100
patients in hospitals helped

63
people found jobs

2,561,614 donated items and services

48,100
clothing items for soldiers, cancer patients, homeless, and orphans

41,150
medical supplies and services provided

1,300
donated bikes with helmets for children who cannot afford them

26
spaces created, including libraries, community gardens, and more

childrensmuseum.org/poca

TABLE OF CONTENTS

FOREWORD

Sometimes we are given opportunities that we don't immediately recognize as gifts. When called upon to take on a new project, we wonder if we have the time, energy, or talent to accept the additional responsibility. The Power of Children Awards program was that gift for me.

I have always believed in having my hands open to the possibilities of life. I have always sincerely loved working with children. One of my passions is finding the best—the hidden talent, the potential, the joy—in the children with whom I have had the pleasure to work. When I was asked to take over the administration of the Power of Children Awards after its inaugural year in 2005, I didn't realize how it would fuel that passion.

Truthfully, even though I was already engrossed in working for The Children's Museum of Indianapolis as the Director of Volunteer Services, I didn't know much about the Power of Children Awards, which we affectionately refer to as POCA. I hadn't yet read the conceptual document, which was based on the vision of creating a forum to recognize the outstanding efforts of young people in philanthropy. It was presented as an extension of the museum's exhibit *The Power of Children*.

While initially concerned about taking on more responsibility, I quickly realized what a gift I'd been handed. POCA makes me feel great joy and gratitude. I was fortunate to have been chosen to do this work, and for that I thank Jeffrey Patchen, President and CEO of the museum, for allowing me to participate in this important initiative.

When I am in a room with the POCA winners and nominees, I feel as if I am in a powerful brain trust in which all things are possible. The passion that each winner has about his or her project is contagious; each one has touched my heart. The privilege to have watched many of the participants' projects take off and flourish has been an honor. Observing the energy, intellect, and spirit of the winners as they propel themselves forward is priceless. It's easy then to know the future of our country is in capable hands.

We have come a long way in 10 years. Through 2014, we have awarded 50 youths the *Power of Children Award*. In 2012, we opened up nominations to a national audience. We continue to seek resources and sponsorship to support and expand POCA to a broader audience.

When you read the POCA recipients' stories, I hope that the enormous positive impact their projects have made will be evident.

This book would not have been possible without Katy Allen, Vice President of Human Resources and Organizational Development, who consistently offered mentorship, leadership, and a willingness to always have my back; Andrew Kimmel, a graduate student intern who shouldered the burden of compiling, researching, interviewing, writing, and rewriting the foundation of this book without complaint; Mary LaVenture, Volunteer Services and POCA Administrator, who patiently endeavored to stay the course even when the obstacles seemed insurmountable; and Jan Nordsiek, Volunteer and Intern Coordinator, who taught us "project management 101" and continued to keep the Volunteer Services ship afloat as we worked to make this book a reality.

I also want to thank Keith Ogorek, Senior Vice President, Marketing at Author Solutions, for his generosity, guidance, and support for this book. It was due to Keith's efforts that the museum was able to partner with Author Solutions, which allowed us to celebrate the 10th anniversary of the Power of Children Awards with a book highlighting the winning projects and the young people who brought them to life.

Finally, the members of the POCA adjudication committee—many of whom have been part of the judging process since the beginning—deserve special recognition for their efforts. To sort through each year's applications, which feature worthy projects by young people around the country, and select the award winners is a responsibility that no one takes lightly. For their dedication and belief in the value of honoring young people involved in community service, all of us at the museum say thank you.

POCA winners embraced their causes and marched into the unknown with their hearts open, intent on making a difference, one person and one cause at a time. They raised money, inspired hundreds of volunteers to join their causes and persevered even when their own families did not quite understand why they were doing what they were doing. They met celebrities, politicians, and presidents, and they started companies, launched websites, and established nonprofit foundations.

Through it all, they remained true to a common goal: to make a difference in someone else's life. They all believed that despite our differences in race, religion, ethnicity, social or economic circumstances, or physical or mental capabilities, everyone deserves respect as a fellow member of the global community.

My hope is that you, the reader, will be compelled to make a difference because of this book—that you will feel inspired to do at least one extraordinary thing to make the world a better place.

Debbie Young
Director of Volunteer Services and
The Power of Children Awards

If you are interested in funding opportunities or applying for the Power of Children Awards, please contact The Children's Museum of Indianapolis.

INTRODUCTION

In 2005 The Children's Museum of Indianapolis opened *The Power of Children*, a permanent exhibit devoted to honoring the lives and legacies of three extraordinary youths: Anne Frank, Ruby Bridges, and Ryan White. None of them chose the circumstances that made them significant figures in 20th-century history. What they did choose was to summon the strength to make a difference.

Anne Frank never intended to be remembered for her diary, a firsthand account of her reactions to the brutality of the Jewish Holocaust. But she wanted to be a writer, and turned her diary into a chronicle of her life while hiding from the Nazis in a building in Amsterdam.

Despite the dire circumstances Anne also wrote about her aspirations, having the courage to dream about what her future might look like. It was a future she never saw, dying in a Nazi concentration camp at age 15 without ever knowing the enormous impact her diary would have on the lives of millions of children and adults for decades to come. Saved by a family friend, Anne's diary was first published in 1947 by her father Otto (the only member of the Frank family to survive). It very quickly became a worldwide best-seller, and in the decades since has remained one of the world's most beloved books, in part because of the courage and hopefulness that Anne conveyed in her writing.

Ruby Bridges never asked to be a central figure in the anguished battle over the racial desegregation of America's public schools. In 1960 she was simply an unassuming 6-year-old who wanted to go to school like any other child. Yet that desire became the basis for Ruby's place in history as the first African American child to integrate an all-white Southern elementary school, William Frantz Elementary School in New Orleans. To be protected from violent protesting mobs, Ruby and her mother had to be escorted to school every day by U.S. Marshals.

The situation didn't make sense to Ruby. At the time, she didn't understand why she had to sit in a classroom all by herself with her teacher, Mrs. Henry. And she wondered why so many people who did not even know her seemed to hate her. She had no idea that artist Norman Rockwell would document her bravery in his painting *The Problem We All Live With* or that she would become a symbol of hope and civil justice. Unlike Anne Frank, Ruby has lived a full life and been able to see the extraordinary impact her experience has had on millions of others.

Ryan White never asked to be the poster boy in the fight against discrimination by an uninformed public against early victims of the HIV/AIDS epidemic. A hemophiliac, Ryan became infected with HIV from a contaminated blood treatment in the mid-1980s. At the time of his diagnosis of AIDS in 1984, little was known about the disease, which had only begun showing up in the United States a few years before. In the small northern Indiana town where Ryan and his family lived, fear of the mysterious disease and lack of knowledge about how it spread led the community to ostracize and isolate the White family. Ryan was asked to leave his school. His family was forced to move.

Fortunately, at a new school in a new town, citizens and school officials took the time to become educated about AIDS, and Ryan was able to go to school and fulfill his dream of being a normal teenager. Ryan's story helped shine a light on bullying and taught many Americans about the importance of compassion for victims of disease and discrimination. By the time he died from AIDS-related complications in 1990, Ryan had become an internationally known advocate for HIV/AIDS education and research.

The experiences of these three young people have inspired millions of people worldwide. Thrown into extraordinary situations, they proved to be extraordinary individuals. As the catalysts for *The Power of Children* exhibit, their stories inspired other children to take action and make a difference in their schools and communities.

Recognizing that, The Children's Museum set out to honor youths in Indiana and beyond who were (and are) making extraordinary differences in the lives of others. With generous gifts from the Deborah Joy Simon Charitable Trust, in 2005 the Power of Children Awards (POCA) began, and the program continues today.

To launch the program the museum invited applications from young people in Grades 6 through 11 who met four criteria. Each one had seen a need, created a project to meet that need, made an impact with the project, and empowered others through the project. To ensure a fair and impartial judging process, the museum asked community leaders and representatives from diverse organizations across Central Indiana to join POCA's adjudication committee. The committee selected four outstanding youths to receive the first Power of Children Awards, which were announced at a simple luncheon.

Over the following years, POCA grew incrementally while the commitment of the judges grew considerably—so much so that many of the founding members remained active on the committee 10 years later. The judges pore over pages of applications from nominees and nominators each year, spending hours completing scoring sheets. Then they meet to share their compiled scores, deliberate over the prospects, and select the winners. Each year, the committee members are humbled by the challenges the nominees overcome and the dedication they display as they strive to make a difference in the lives of others in the spirit of Anne Frank, Ruby Bridges, and Ryan White.

Though they began with a focus on Indiana youths, The Power of Children Awards expanded to welcome applicants from throughout the United States in 2012. By 2014, awards had been given to a total of 50 recipients from 33 cities in 11 states, and their projects had touched 57 countries. More than 54,356 volunteers and 59 businesses had been inspired to help with projects, and the 50 winners had collectively raised more than $10 million for their projects.

POCA recipients receive scholarships they can use to attend Indiana University–Purdue University Indianapolis (IUPUI), the University of Indianapolis, or Butler University. In addition, they receive a $2,000 grant to invest in their projects, and they are featured in the *The Power of Children* exhibit at The Children's Museum.

POCA winners also are invited to participate in the annual Power of Children Symposium at the museum. This one-day event brings youths in Grades 5 through 10 to discover, discuss, and explore opportunities for continuing to make a difference in their communities and states as well as in the nation and the world.

As you read the profiles of the POCA recipients that follow, keep this in mind: The desire to help others is a basic human trait. When combined with the energy, focus, and drive of young people, the results are often powerful projects that have a positive impact on everyone involved.

It's the young people behind such projects that The Power of Children Awards honor. Whether their projects are local, national, or international in scope, the POCA recipients all share one thing in common. Each of them identified a need and stepped up to meet it.

These young people weren't thinking about awards or recognition. They were doing what they felt needed to be done. They were trying to help, sometimes when no one else would. They were trying to make a difference in the lives of other human beings. That's compassion in action.

The Power of Children Awards were created to celebrate those selfless acts of generosity that are so often overlooked because they're done by young people—the very same young people who will one day be running the world. By recognizing their contributions while they're still young, The Children's Museum of Indianapolis hopes to instill in the award recipients the sense that doing good things is a valuable way to spend their time and energy, and that by trying to make a difference they set an example worthy of recognition, repetition, and replication.

The Awards name says it all: The Power of Children. It's a power that, if harnessed and directed, can change the world for the better.

~ ~ ~

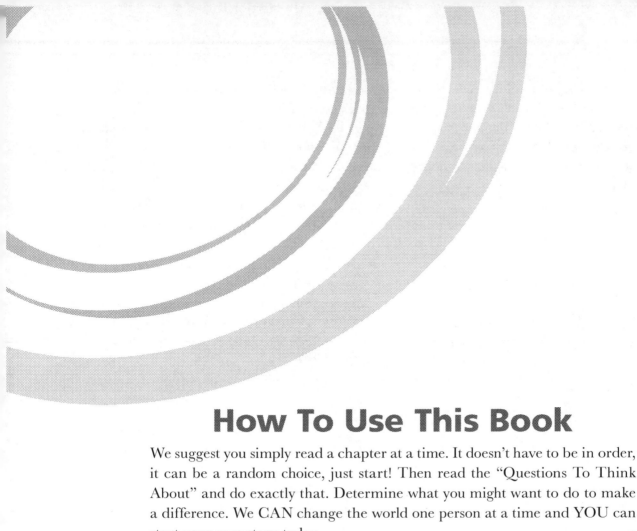

How To Use This Book

We suggest you simply read a chapter at a time. It doesn't have to be in order, it can be a random choice, just start! Then read the "Questions To Think About" and do exactly that. Determine what you might want to do to make a difference. We CAN change the world one person at a time and YOU can start your own story today.

TRAILBLAZERS

Two hundred years ago people began to filter out of the original 13 states and head westward across America. They often followed crude paths created by the explorers who preceded them. Those explorers were trailblazers, because they actually blazed (created) trails where none existed before. They also took on the challenges that came with being the first to forge ahead into unknown territory.

The young people profiled in the following pages all took on challenges that led them where few have gone before. Whether feeding the homeless, speaking up for victims of bullying, helping communities affected by natural disasters, working on behalf of children with autism, providing aide to U.S. soldiers, giving electric wheelchairs to people with disabilities, or offering healthcare and job opportunities to people around the world, these Power of Children Awards recipients serve as inspiration! They blazed trails where none existed.

These extraordinary youth have demonstrated how far compassion, conviction, and courage can take us on behalf of issues important to us. They led the way from the darkness of doing nothing into the light of doing something meaningful on behalf of others. They did great things that changed lives, boosted spirits, and improved futures for everyone who benefited from their efforts. Their stories clearly tell us: "If I can do it, so can you." We all have the power to blaze trails of our own.

~ ~ ~

DANIEL KENT (2005)

"Work to develop an insatiable curiosity about all that is around you. The more you learn and discover, the more you will see opportunities to help make a difference in your community."

Project: Net Literacy

- Established in 2003
- Attracted 3,500 volunteers by 2014
- Repurposed 28,000 computers by 2014
- Gave 250,000 people access to digital information by 2014
- Provided $1,200,000 in services annually by 2014

Daniel stands outside in New Haven, Connecticut, where he attended Yale University.

Daniel Kent was a man on a mission. In high school, he learned that senior citizens had no programs that taught them how to use computers or access information on the Internet. Since senior citizens sometimes have difficulty getting around or getting reliable transportation to places outside of their homes, Daniel realized that teaching them to use technology could help them feel more independent and less isolated from family and friends.

To develop his idea, Daniel used $4,000 he had saved for a car to establish a nonprofit organization called Senior Connects. In addition to collecting donations of money and computers, he asked people to repair the computers for seniors to use. At one point after a computer drive, his parents' family room was filled with more than 100 computers. Volunteers also taught seniors such basic skills as how to use email and social media to stay in touch with people who were important to them.

Eventually Senior Connects grew larger and larger. Daniel used his $2,000 Power of Children grant to fix 130 computers for seniors in need. He also kept looking for more ways to help more people. Little by little, he pushed the project to start new programs. By 2014 he was the executive director of Net Literacy, an umbrella organization that includes Senior Connects as one of its programs.

Net Literacy educates students and parents about safe Internet use through a program called Safe Connects. Another program, Community Connects, increases computer access for underserved communities. High school students learn about money management through Financial Connects. Net Literacy also encourages students to refurbish computers through Computer Connects. Those refurbished computers

As an inaugural POCA winner in 2005, Daniel spoke at the 10th Anniversary Awards event.

re used in the Safe Connects and Senior Connects programs.

Net Literacy has been a student-run organization since Daniel started it. Because students run the organization, they learn firsthand how to find new ways to volunteer and help people in their communities.

As an advocate for the use of technology, Daniel met with representatives of such well-known companies as Google, Intel, Dell, and Cisco, as well as with members of Congress and White House staff. Because of his hard work more people have access to personal computers. More important, they have a better understanding of how to use them. His work earned him the Computerworld 21st Century Achievement Award in Digital Inclusion and the Google Zeitgeist Young Minds Award, as well as the President's Volunteer Service Award.

This passion for technology has carried over into Daniel's personal life. His goal is to expand Net Literacy while exploring the quickly changing world of technology. At Haverford College in Pennsylvania, Daniel studied how cities grow and work before moving to Yale University in Connecticut for a graduate degree in marketing and strategy. He also completed a year-long internship with LegalZoom in California.

The Power of Children Award helped the Net Literacy team increase awareness of the digital inclusion problem that affects communities nationwide, Daniel noted. "It allowed Net Literacy to provide computers to individuals and groups who were previously on the wrong side of the digital divide."

Daniel makes a presentation at the Yale School of Management. He is an advocate for smart technology use.

QUESTIONS TO THINK ABOUT

- Have you ever taught someone older than yourself a new skill? How did teaching what you know improve your own skill?
- What kinds of technology do you use? How did you learn how to use them? What are some things you can teach others about the technology you know how to use?
- Ask your teachers and family members about technology that was popular when they were your age. How has that technology changed over time? Why is it different now? How do you think technology will change as you get older?
- Do you know how a computer works? Write a paragraph explaining how it works to someone who does not know. If you can explain a concept to someone, it shows that you really know your stuff!

WESTON LUZADDER (2007)

"Follow your instincts, welcome the unknown, and go boldly into the future."

Project: Bikes 4 Kids

- Established in 2006
- Gave out 1,300 bikes and helmets to children and adults
- Donated bikes to schools, libraries, and charities

Weston Luzadder loved bicycles. He spent hours riding his bike, repairing bikes in his garage, and working at a bike shop. At his high school in Carmel, Indiana, he noticed that many of the other students didn't have bikes of their own. Since he had so much fun with his, he decided he should do something so others could enjoy bikes, too.

Weston received a scholarship at Marian University in Indianapolis, Indiana, as a member of the university's cycling team.

The result was Bikes 4 Kids, an organization that Weston founded in 2006. In the beginning Weston asked people to donate used or broken bicycles that they did not ride anymore. He then fixed them and gave them to kids without bikes. The cost was just a little time and effort, and about $35 in repair costs for each bike. But the excitement in a child's eyes when he delivered a bike was reward enough for Weston.

Weston founded his project 2006 and won his award in 20

In addition to their new bikes, Weston gave every child a helmet. He then took a picture of them with their new bikes. Later, he sent them a note with the picture and a friendly reminder to wear their helmets. Each child who received a bike had an open invitation to contact Weston if anything ever went wrong with a bike.

At Carmel High School Weston also created a club to get more people involved in Bikes 4 Kids. Members worked together to clean and fix bikes. While they worked, they learned more about bike maintenance.

Weston didn't realize his project would affect more people than the ones who received bikes. Often other students came up to him and said they wanted to start their own projects, most of which had nothing to do with bikes. Inspired by what Weston had done, they figured they could do something to help others too.

Because buying helmets, new tires, and other replacement parts cost money, Weston was happy to win the Power of Children Award. He used the $2,000 grant to purchase the supplies he needed to make bicycling safe and fun for the young people who received bikes from Bikes 4 Kids.

After high school Weston went to Marian University in Indianapolis, Indiana, where he received a scholarship as a member of the university's cycling team. He majored in economics and also collected money to provide bicycles to Africa through the international program World Bicycle Relief. He graduated from Marian in 2013 and landed a job selling bicycle parts for a company in Utah.

Though Weston moved out of Indiana, his parents continued to run Bikes 4 Kids, keeping their son's dream to make bikes available to as many young riders as possible.

QUESTIONS TO THINK ABOUT

- Do you own a bike? If so, how often do you ride it? Do you wear a helmet?
- Why do you ride your bike? Are there benefits or risks to riding a bike that are different from using a car or public transportation?
- Have you ever had to repair a bike? What did you need to fix?
- Have you ever raced your bike to raise money for charity?
- Would you ever let someone borrow your bike if he or she didn't have one?

AMANDA & GRANT MANSARD (2008)

"Every young person has the ability to create change and impact his or her community."

−Amanda Mansard

"Nothing is unattainable in life! Set your goals as high as you can imagine reaching, then soar past them."

−Grant Mansard

Project: Youth Embracing Service (YES)
- Established in 2007
- 26,000 hours of work by volunteers
- 3,400 Christmas cards to Indiana soldiers overseas
- 180 volunteers delivered hugs to individuals battling terminal diseases
- 100 homecare patients received Easter baskets

Sometimes what appears to be a problem is actually an opportunity. It just depends on how you look at it. In 2007 Amanda and Grant Mansard's father was injured at work. Worried about him as he recovered, the Mansards searched for something to keep them occupied. Believing in the value of serving others and realizing that doing so might also help them, Amanda and Grant created Youth Embracing Service (YES), a nonprofit organization that provided young people with volunteer opportunities throughout their hometown of Terre Haute, Indiana.

Amanda and Grant started YES, an organization that inspired volunteers to give 26,000 hours of their time to help others.

Amanda and Grant discovered that there weren' many organizations in their community that actively sought young people as volunteers. YES changed that. Since Amanda and Grant both felt rewarded by doing service projects, they set out to show other young people how to start their own. The Mansards felt the success of YES would encourage the development of additional projects, which in turn would help many more people. By teaching their peers how to help those in need, Amanda and Grant wanted to inspire them to continue to do so throughout their lives.

Amanda shows the wild side volunteerin

In the beginning it was easy enough. The Mansards called various organizations to ask about volunteer opportunities. As it turned out, there were plenty. However, getting the word out to young people was something most organizations didn't know how to do. Amanda and Grant offered to pass along the information.

Because they wanted YES to attract donors, Amanda and Grant filled out the paperwork to make YES a nonprofit organization, which meant that people who made donations might get a break on their tax returns. They also created YES projects and invited young people to help complete them. What was unique about YES, though, was the fact that it gave young people the resources they needed to start their own projects.

It helped them identify where help was needed, develop plans to address those needs, and find funds for their projects. The Mansards mentored young people during project planning and connected them to resources they could use to make their projects work.

Amanda and Grant used their Power of Children grant to launch more service projects and expand the ones already under way. Winning the Power of Children Award also led them to a new project. They teamed up with 2009 winner Kaylee Shirrell to help with her project Hats of Hope (see the Helpers section for details).

As of 2014 YES was still going strong, and Amanda and Grant were still dedicated to its success, while also preparing themselves for the future. Grant was a student at Indiana State University in Terre Haute majoring in nursing. Having headed the North American food drive for two years, his goal was to become the CEO of a hospital one day.

A Lilly Endowment scholar, Amanda was studying at Butler University in Indianapolis, majoring in science, technology, and society (STS) with minors in healthcare management and French. Like her brother, she wanted to continue to help people in need, ultimately working for a hospital or other nonprofit. Amanda and Grant believed in the power of young people to have a big impact on the lives of others. They encouraged their peers to check out service organizations in their hometowns or go to national sites online to find out what they could do to help others.

Amanda and Grant Mansard celebrate their addition to the Power of Children gallery.

QUESTIONS TO THINK ABOUT

- Have you ever asked your brother or sister (or another family member) to join you on a volunteer project?
- When something makes you worried, what do you do to make yourself feel better? Have you tried volunteering?
- What current needs do you see in your community? How do you think you could address those needs?
- Do you know of ways you can raise money or resources to help others?

ALISON MANSFIELD (2008)

"Dream big, share your passion, learn from others, and strive to make a difference."

Project: Operation U.S. Troop Support

- Established in 2005
- Collected and distributed 8,000 letters, 13,000 pairs of wool socks, and 96,000 toiletries, snacks, and small toys for Afghan and Iraqi children
- Raised $300,000 in donated items, cash, and volunteer time
- Provided socks for 19% of all soldiers serving in Afghanistan
- Inspired others to collect and donate items

Alison went on to study English Yale Universi

Afghanistan is a country of extremes. In part it's a desert, with scorching sun and sweltering temperatures. In the summer in some Afghan cities the temperature is often over 100 degrees. But in northern Afghanistan, where there are mountain ranges, frigid cold is more common. In those regions wool socks are precious commodities. Alison Mansfield, a 5th-grader in Fort Wayne, Indiana, learned that surprising fact in 2005, as a result of her friendship with a U.S. soldier.

That friendship began with a sermon at the church her family attended. When the pastor described how Sergeant Paul Statzer had been gravely injured in a roadside explosion, Alison was moved by his patriotism and pride. That led her to conduct a telephone interview with Sergeant Statzer for a school essay.

After the interview Alison wanted to meet the sergeant in person, so she and her mother flew to Washington, D.C., to visit him at Walter Reed Army Medical Center, where he was recuperating. During the flight, Alison asked other passengers on the flight to write letters of appreciation to wounded soldiers. By the time the plane landed Alison had 115 letters, which she delivered to Sergeant Statzer and other soldiers who were recovering from their injuries.

At that moment, Alison's nonprofit organization Operation U.S. Troop Support was born. She created a variety of military support projects to aid soldiers. Alison collected letters of appreciation to raise soldiers' morale. She also sent them toiletries and snacks. It was on a trip to the post office to mail those supplies, though, that she learned the importance of socks. A postal clerk with a family member serving in Afghanistan told her about the soldiers' need for warm, dry feet in the cold, snowy mountains.

Alison then created the Operation Socks for Our Troops project as part of her larger nonprofit organization. She set a modest goal of collecting between 500 and 1,000 pairs of socks for troops in Afghanistan and Iraq. By 2008, Operation Socks for Our Troops

Alison stands beside a military Humvee. She provided more than 100,000 items for Afghan and Iraqi children and United States soldiers stationed overseas.

ad collected and delivered more than 5,000 pairs. News media and other organizations took notice and were inspired to start collections of their own.

One middle school student was inspired to collect 500 pairs of socks after hearing Alison's story. The director of student wellness at Purdue University in West Lafayette, Indiana also vowed to raise money and collect socks on campus for her project, telling her: "My father's feet froze when he was a prisoner of war in Germany in World War II. I know he would be very proud of you!" The Power of Children Award gave Alison a $2,000 grant, which she used to help cover the cost of shipping all those socks overseas.

Alison also received letters of gratitude from the soldiers who received the socks and other supplies she sent. "In this environment, we forget that there are even weekends and holidays," one soldier in the U.S. Army's 82nd Airborne Division wrote. "We forget that there are *off* times and we sometimes lose focus of life in general back home. So again, thank you for bringing me back to reality and making me smile, if even for a moment."

Operation U.S. Troop Support continued to expand as Alison tackled more projects. As an English major at Yale University in New Haven Connecticut, she continued to work on behalf of U.S. troops through her organization. In addition to aiding troops, Operation U.S. Troop Support sent toys and educational supplies to Afghan children.

Alison also became interested in addressing the needs of soldiers' families, who make sacrifices at home while the troops serve overseas. That led her to widen her focus, and as of 2014 she had more projects on the horizon. Winner of numerous awards for her service projects, Alison is an example of the fact that sometimes the simplest things have the biggest impact.

As part of Alison's project, she sent homemade Valentines to the troops.

QUESTIONS TO THINK ABOUT
- Do you know anyone who has served in the military? What did that person need while away from home?
- Do you know anyone who has family serving in the military now? What do they do while their family member is away from home?
- How could you inspire people who believe in causes to volunteer their time?

JACOB BALDWIN (2009)

"The project you are working on will only have as much persistence and endurance as you do, if you are the leader."

Project: Project K.I.D./Operation Safeguard
- Established in 2009
- Raised $3,000 to create a Playcare kit at Riverview Hospital
- Designed a play-area fence that can be easily stored and assembled
- Developed partnerships among local and healthcare organizations
- Coordinated training to prepare volunteers for disasters
- Wrote a user's guide for Playcare kits

Jacob relaxing and working in Br[...]

When disasters strike, no one helps more quickly than first responders. The police, paramedics, and firefighters who are the first ones to disaster areas are also called first responders. Certified first responders can be everyday people who have special qualifications to help in disasters. They know CPR, how to set bones, and how to use some medical equipment. Their careers are spent being trained to help those in need. However, disasters come at unexpected times.

When Jacob Baldwin began volunteering in disaster preparedness exercises, he learned about Project K.I.D., an organization that provides childcare for children affected by disasters. The organization was founded to help children affected by the most destructive storm in U.S. history, Hurricane Katrina in 2005. Project K.I.D. also provides training for youths who want to know how to help in disaster situations.

Project K.I.D. created Playcare kits. Stored in hospitals and schools, the kits consist of six boxes and contain everything from blankets and first aid supplies to toys and coloring books. They also provide a safe enclosure for children which includes fencing. The fencing can be quickly assembled and easily installed at a site. First responders can use the enclosures to give their own children and those affected by disaster a safe place. Children are safe while their parents help people in need of assistance.

Jacob saw the need to integrate Project K.I.D.'s resources into h[...] local community. Noticing that his Indiana commu[...]nity did not have programs to train youth in disaste[...] preparation or kits to provide care for children in th[...] aftermath of disasters, Jacob wrote grant applicatio[...] that raised $3,000 to provide a complete Playcare k[...] for Riverview Hospital in Noblesville, Indiana.

But Jacob initially noticed that the fencing tha[...] Project K.I.D. used was hard to assemble. It als[...] could not be used on many surfaces. So he designe[...] a portable, lightweight system that could be easil[...] stored and assembled. He organized a team to hel[...] build the new fencing, creating five new fences to b[...] used around Indiana.

Jacob also co-founded a week-long camp fo[...] youths called Operation Safeguard to teach the pa[...] ticipants what to do in the event of a disaster. Jaco[...] hosted the first Operation Safeguard camp at Pa[...]

cob graduated from high school and received
four-year scholarship from the University of
orth Carolina, Chapel Hill.

Tudor School in Indianapolis. The program, which attracted 38 middle school and high school students, was so successful that the Federal Emergency Management Agency (FEMA) considered it as a model for national replication.

Because of the attention he received as a Power of Children Award recipient, Jacob was able get more people involved in his projects. That allowed him to send a PlayCare kit to Haiti following the massive earthquake near Port-au-Prince in 2010. Jacob's kit, which he made sure was filled with needed supplies, provided welcome relief to some of the hundreds of thousands of people who were affected.

A Gold Medal Congressional Award winner, Jacob received a four-year scholarship to attend the University of North Carolina at Chapel Hill. In the future he hoped to run a business focused on treating its customers and employees well. He planned to make service a part of whatever he did in the future.

QUESTIONS TO THINK ABOUT

- Does your family have an emergency plan? What would you do if you were separated from each other when a disaster happens?
- What sort of natural disasters might happen near you? How can you help prepare yourself and others?
- What do you think you could do to help young children affected by disasters?
- Do you know CPR or first aid? Where could you learn about these in your community?

OLIVIA RUSK (2009)

"Don't be afraid to put your project out there. What has happened . . . has been amazing."

Project: Olivia's Cause

- Established in 2008
- Created an inspirational music video
- Received national media attention
- Presented motivational speeches at schools

Do you know someone—maybe a family member, maybe a classmate, maybe a friend—whom others perceive as "different"? If so, you know that being different can make a person a target of teasing or bullying, even though being different makes that individual unique and wonderful.

Olivia Rusk is one of those unique and wonderful people. When she was 18 months old, Olivia lost all of her hair. When her mother took her to the doctor, she discovered that Olivia had a condition called alopecia.

Our bodies have defenses called immune systems to protect us from getting sick. Our immune systems attack bacteria and viruses that come into our bodies. Sometimes a person's immune system cannot tell the difference between something bad and something good. When this happens, the person is said to have an autoimmune disease. In Olivia's case, her immune system attacked her hair.

Alopecia affects nearly 2 percent of all Americans. It's hard to predict if and when a person's hair will grow back. Some end up with bald spots. Some lose all of their hair on their heads. Some even lose their eyebrows and eyelashes.

Olivia and her doctors worked together and found a treatment that caused her hair to grow back. But when she was 8 years old Olivia lost her hair again. Concerned about taking any more medicine to treat her condition, she ordered a wig. She liked the idea of picking out a new hairstyle, and at first she loved her wig.

But Olivia liked to run and play, and her wig made her head feel itchy and hot. One day, as she was getting ready for school, Olivia announced she was no longer going to wear her wig. It was a brave and bold decision for a 3rd-grader to make. Her mother was concerned that the other children in her class would react negatively. But Olivia's confidence and the willingness of her teacher to explain her condition to her classmates made it a lot easier.

Olivia continues to inspire others with alopecia to just be themselves

As Olivia grew older, she reflected on what it meant to be herself. Instead of trying to be who other people thought she should be, she wanted to be who she actually was. She knew that wasn't always an easy thing to do. Through connections she'd made by attending support groups, she'd met many people who'd had bad experiences with others who'd picked on them for being different.

In order to raise awareness about alopecia and to encourage people with alopecia to be themselves, Olivia wrote, filmed, and produced a music video called *I Could Be Great!* To overcome the financial and technical hurdles of such a big project, she partnered with the Indiana University–Purdue University Indianapolis (IUPUI) Media Center. The project was sponsored by a local hair salon that helped design the set and pay for the production.

The video featured Olivia being bullied in school for her appearance. One day, as she is out shopping for clothes with her friends, two talent scouts for a model agency discover her. The video ends with Olivia being featured at a runway style show.

Posted on YouTube and sites that support people with alopecia, the video has been seen by thousands of viewers around the world. Many wrote to Olivia to thank her for raising awareness of the condition and for inspiring them to be themselves. One viewer in Australia wrote that after watching the video she decided to take off her wig, too.

Olivia continued to inspire others by becoming a motivational speaker and writing a book about her experience. She was featured on television programs, including *The Today Show* on NBC. Olivia's Cause, the nonprofit organization that she and her mother established, continues to raise awareness about alopecia and encourage kids with the condition to be themselves. Olivia credited the Power of Children Award for inspiring her to share her story with more people.

Olivia posing with her leaf in the Power of Children Gallery at the awards ceremony in 2009.

QUESTIONS TO THINK ABOUT

- Have you ever been teased about your appearance or actions? How did it make you feel?
- What would you do for someone else who had been bullied?
- What challenges have you overcome that could inspire others?
- Have you ever given a speech? How do you think you can share inspirational stories with others?
- Do you like doing art, acting, or making videos? How could you use those skills to help others?

JORDYN BEVER (2010)

"Many people have told me that my small group has changed their views on people who have disabilities, and that's what it takes to make a change: one person or one thing at a time and it all adds up!"

Project: Destiny Color Guard

- Established in 2008
- 14 members in the group
- 25 volunteers involved
- Received $1,900 United Way grant

For hundreds of years armies have included color guards—literally soldiers in charge of protecting the colors, or flag, that represented the castle, kingdom, or country for which they were fighting. Today's equivalent of colors are the young people twirling and tossing flags in step with a marching band. For Jordyn Bever, participating in Greenfield Central High School's color guard was one of the high points in her life.

Jordyn believes that everyone should be viewed for who they are.

Believing that everyone should be viewed for who they are rather than for what they've overcome, Jordyn was inspired by a color guard from another high school that featured members with special needs. As a result she created Destiny Color Guard.

Open to students in Grades 6 through 12 serve by Hancock South Madison Joint Services i Greenfield, Indiana, Destiny Color Guard require a year to plan and organize. Jordyn, who was i 8th grade at the time, wanted to make sure she wa working with the students in an appropriate manne so she met with her school's special education teach ers to get advice on the best way to teach the colo guard routines.

With the help of grants and the input of the mem bers' parents, Destiny Color Guard became a popula program within the community. It also became on of only three color guards like it in the nation. No only did it provide special needs students a means t build confidence and pride in their abilities, it als changed the way other people viewed them.

As Destiny's members learned and practiced the routines, they started performing at basketball game and marching band events. They impressed everyon around them. Other students (and adults) no longe saw them as people who were different or had limita tions but as individuals who could master difficult challenges if given the opportunity. Parents and Destiny members alike were proud of what they had accomplished.

Jordyn graduated from high school in 2013 and used her Power of

Jordyn conducts a drill with s of her color guard memb

Children Award scholarship to attend the University of Indianapolis, where she worked on a degree in biology in preparation for medical school and a career as a pediatrician. But she remained committed to Destiny, training other people to work with the group when she couldn't.

Though busy with her studies and the university's Symphonic Wind Ensemble, Jordyn regularly commuted to Greenfield for practice sessions as well as to organize volunteers and schedule performances. She used her Power of Children grant to buy the group a new sound system and design a website.

Jordyn, who did a presentation about Destiny Color Guard at a National Collegiate Honors Conference, later remarked that she would love to be able to help every school in the country have a similar group. Though sometimes it seemed to her that her project was too small to make a difference, after six seasons Jordyn knew she had made people re-evaluate their views of those with special needs.

QUESTIONS TO THINK ABOUT

- Do you have a disability or know someone who does? How does it affect your life or that person's life?
- Teachers go through a lot of training to understand how people learn. What do you think Jordyn had to know about as she taught routines to others?
- Do you see projects that others are doing that inspire you?
- How can you do a project that is slightly different from the ones already out there?
- Have you ever wanted to join a group but could not? Why couldn't you? How did you feel about your experience?

JARED BROWN (2010)

"Just because an issue appears to be impossible to overcome doesn't mean there's nothing that can be done about it."

Project: Autism Sensory Kits

- Established in 2008
- Attracted 150 volunteers
- Raised $4,300

Autism affects one out of every 68 children born in the United States. Many people affected by autism have difficulties interacting with others and understanding nonverbal forms of communication, such as facial expressions and gestures. Many, however, have great abilities in visual, musical, and academic skills. It all depends on the individual.

Jared Brown, a freshman at Warren Central High School in Indianapolis, Indiana, was personally acquainted with autism. As one of the millions diagnosed with the condition, he had struggled throughout his life to deal with social situations and learning challenges. So when it came time as a Boy Scout to undertake a project that would help others, he decided to draw on personal experience.

While people with autism are unique in the types of challenges each faces, they often share difficulties in communicating with and relating to others. When Jared was a kindergartener, his teacher gave him a sensory toy that allowed him to play while refocusing his attention. Depending on the individual, a sensory toy can calm or stimulate. In either case the goal is to help that person be successful in the classroom.

Appreciating how his teacher went out of her way to help him, Jared wanted to give other children the same experience. He began researching homemade sensory kits. He found out that no one had ever created a complete kit that met the needs of children with autism and attention deficit hyperactivity disorder (ADHD).

Jared set out to create his own Autism Sensory Kits. He looked for items that were easy and inexpensive to make. The kit he finally developed included weighted Sockpals, fidget toys, and flip charts.

Like sock puppets, Sockpals are socks that have been filled with soft material and have faces drawn on sewn on them. Autistic students use them as calming toys, much like stress balls.

Jared oversees the delivery of sensory ki

Similarly, fidget toys are used to help decrease stress, increase the awareness of the sense of touch, and keep students' hands busy while they are doing something static like waiting in line. A Rubik's Cube™ would be considered a fidget toy.

Because people with autism may have trouble communicating their emotions to those around them, flip charts show the names of various emotions and a picture of a face depicting each one. Students can flip through

...he charts to find an image that ...presents how they are feeling.

To raise funds to build the ...its, Jared applied for a United ...Way grant and asked for dona...ions. He knew that he had to ...vercome some of his personal ...hallenges to be successful. But ...o help those he wanted to help, ...e knew he had to motivate and ...ad others, which meant he had ...o step outside his comfort zone.

By doing so, he turned a ...ood idea into a big success— ...nd earned the Boy Scouts' top ...anking of Eagle Scout. His sen...ory kits eventually were used in ...ve school systems. Jared went ...n to create a DVD that helped ...udents understand appropriate ...ocial behaviors.

Jared turned a good idea into a big success and earned the Boy Scout's top ranking of Eagle Scout.

The teachers who received the sensory kits raved about how useful they were. In 2014, six years after he started his project, Jared still heard from school systems throughout Indiana wanting information on how to make sensory kits of their own.

Following his 2011 graduation from Warren Central, Jared used his Power of Children scholarship to attend Indiana University–Purdue University Indianapolis (IUPUI), majoring in New Media. A member of the university's honor society, he was involved in a virtual reality project that helped bring history to life. After graduation he wanted to continue working in the fields of digital storytelling and animation.

QUESTIONS TO THINK ABOUT

- Autism is just one kind of condition that can affect social interaction and communication. What are some others?
- Do you know someone with autism? What are some things you have in common with them?
- What are some things you might consider fidget toys? Do you have any of your own?
- What do you do to concentrate on important tasks? What service project could you do to help others with concentration problems?

TIM BALZ (2012)

"Do not wait for opportunities to present themselves; seek them out."

Project: Freedom Chairs of Indiana

- Established in 2011
- Received $50,000 from 5-Hour Energy Drink
- Dedicated over 1,000 hours of time annually
- Donated 80 wheelchairs

When Tim Balz, a junior at Plainfield High School in Plainfield, Indiana, saw one of his classmates use a manual wheelchair every day, he was puzzled. Why, he wondered, didn't the guy use an electric wheelchair to make it easier to get around?

When Tim asked a special education teacher about his classmate, he discovered the young man's family couldn't afford an electric wheelchair. The teacher explained that with an electric wheelchair, the student's mental and physical skills would improve.

So Tim, a robotics fan, started tinkering. A neighbor had given him a broken wheelchair to use for parts for a robot. Instead of salvaging parts from it as he had planned to do, Tim tried repairing it. In the process he became friends with the student in the wheelchair.

Though Tim wasn't able to fix the wheelchair

Tim's friend, Aaron, with his wheelchair that was specially designed so he could play basketball. Before Tim and his organization customized the chair, Aaron sat on the sidelines.

he had, he was determined to help. He began looking online for an electric wheelchair. When he found one he didn't have enough money to purchase it, so he traded his electric scooter for the wheelchair.

The student volunteers stop their hard work to pose for a picture at the Freedom Chairs storage unit.

Then Tim went to work, modifying the wheelchair for his classmate. One of the toughest things to do was to rewire it. His friend was left-handed, and the chair was built for a right-handed person. But Tim worked every day after school so the chair would be ready in time for graduation ceremonies.

With his new wheelchair, Tim's friend became more independent. Because he no longer had to rely on someone else pushing him in a manual chair it was easier for him to get around, to do his job, and to interact with his doctors and family.

Motivated by the change he saw in his friend, Tim realized that there were others like his classmate who also could benefit from having an electric wheelchair, but didn't have the means to pay for one. Freedom Chairs of Indiana was born. Within a year of creating the organization, Tim had donated chairs to 30 people, improving their lives in the process.

The Power of Children Award grant allowed Tim to pay for a storage space for the wheelchairs people donated to him. He also spent some of the money on new batteries for the chairs. In 2014, he continued to refurbish wheelchairs and head up Freedom Chairs as he completed his degree in mechanical engineering at Rose-Hulman Institute of Technology in Terre Haute, Indiana.

Recipient of a Red Cross Hall of Fame Award, Tim had already taken part in one project that resulted in a patent at Rose-Hulman, and he had big plans for the future. He intended to create his own wheelchair company, making more affordable wheelchairs. No one should be denied the freedom of mobility, he asserted, and wheelchairs can always be improved to give the people who use them the most flexibility possible.

That was in keeping with his belief that working to make even a small impact on a big issue is a help. "If you help to improve just one person's life," he said, "then it is worth it." He had learned that lesson one wheelchair at a time.

Tim was invited to throw the first pitch at an Indianapolis Indians game.

QUESTIONS TO THINK ABOUT

- Are you good with electronics? If so, what do you tinker with? If not, how could you learn those skills?
- Do you like to make new things? Do you always try to come up with a better way to do something?
- Do you think people throw away things and buy new replacements or do people repair things more today? Explain your answer.
- Do you know anyone with a physical disability? What similarities do you have with this person?
- Take a look in your living room, kitchen, garage, or other places in your home. What tools do people use that make their lives easier?

NICHOLAS CLIFFORD (2012)

"You can do more than you ever would have thought if you apply your time correctly."

Project: Employment Barrier Buster

- Established in 2011
- Provided training and moral support to people who were unemployed
- Helped 56 people receive stable jobs
- Collected work clothing to support three employment programs
- Developed an agricultural learning center

In 2008, the U.S. economy took a sudden and disastrous downturn. At least 2.6 million people lost their jobs because the companies they worked for could no longer afford to pay them. That was the most jobs lost in one year since 1945. People needed help to find new jobs or get training to prepare them for new professions.

By 2011 the economy had improved, but a lot of people were still struggling to find jobs and coping with how being unemployed affected what others thought about them. Because of Nicholas Clifford's efforts, many individuals got an opportunity to get jobs and job training, which then changed other people's perceptions of them.

Nicholas, a 7th-grader at St. Thomas Aquina School in Indianapolis, Indiana, created his project Employment Barrier Buster, because he was concerned

The greenhouse was built. Besides agricultural awarene Nicholas helped 56 people obtain employme

about the large number of military veterans who were unemployed. He thought that people who sacrificed so much to serve their country should have opportunities to provide for themselves. Self-sufficiency, Nicholas realized, was the greatest gift he could give others. His project eventually expanded beyond veterans to people from all walks of life. If there was a barrier keeping them from getting a job, Nicholas wanted to help.

To get started Nicholas worked on identifying the resources he and the unemployed could access. He met with staff members from job training programs to figure out what type of assistance people needed. What he discovered was that many job seekers were also struggling with obstacles such as homelessness, physical or emotional disabilities, poor work histories, or criminal records. Nicholas wanted to help them overcome whatever was making their job searches more difficult.

Nicholas examines plans for a new greenhouse. The creation of an agricultural learning center helps people learn skills to become self-sufficient.

What amazed many people about Nicholas's project was how easy it was for a middle-school student to help adults get a job. He knew that job applicants needed work experience in order to get interviews. To provide that experience, he collected materials for job training classes, such as mechanical things that needed to be repaired. He knew that people had to be properly dressed for job interviews, so he arranged for clothing donations to provide interview outfits and work clothes. Nicholas also teamed up with a lawyer who donated his time to help people resolve any legal problems they had.

holas started his
ject when he was in
e seventh grade.

Feeling he still wasn't doing enough, Nicholas brought homemade food to feed people participating in his program because it's hard for someone who's hungry to concentrate on a job search. He also wanted to praise success so he organized a ceremony in the fall and spring to recognize every person who got a job.

Because of Nicholas, many people found stable employment. Among them was a veteran with mental health issues who was hired by another veteran's family-owned business. Then there was the grandmother who, after being released from prison, changed her life by getting a job with a hotel that later named her Employee of the Month twice.

Nicholas, as a freshman at North Central High School in Indianapolis, Indiana in 2014, continued to look for ways to make lives better. He participated in events that raised suicide prevention awareness and collected clothing for various nonprofit organizations. He hoped to expand his Employment Barrier Buster project. Using his Power of Children Awards grant he planned to team up with Kheprw Institute (KI) EcoCenter to build an agricultural learning center and to provide more community events and learning opportunities for people in Indianapolis.

A cross-country runner, Nicholas said that his long-term plans included working in a profession that would allow him to continue helping others in need. In other words, he was in community service for the long run.

QUESTIONS TO THINK ABOUT

- If someone makes a mistake, do they deserve a second chance? A third chance? A fourth? Why do people make mistakes? Have you made mistakes in your life?
- Do you know someone who has lost a job? What happened when they were not employed?
- What skills do you think are necessary to get a good job? Why? Discuss what you think with someone who has a job.
- What steps are you taking now to ensure that you get a good job later? Can you teach others how to take these steps?
- What is an "employment barrier"? How can you help someone who has barriers find employment?

NEHA GUPTA (2012)

"Choose a cause that YOU are passionate about and make an impact."

Project: Empower Orphans
- Established in 2009
- Created five libraries with 15,500 books
- Founded a sewing center with 60 sewing machines
- Raised over $1,300,000 in aid
- Affected the lives of 25,000 children

Neha Gupta comes from a long line of social activists. Her maternal great-great-grandmother worked with Mahatma Gandhi to free India from Great Britain's rule. Her father's family helped feed and educate children in an orphanage in their hometown in India.

Neha was 9 years old when she started volunteering at an orphanage while visiting her grandparents in India. Through that experience she began to understand what orphans there faced. They couldn't afford to go to school, had no access to medical care, and had no families or homes to return to.

They also lived in fear of turning 16, the age when they had to leave the orphanage. Having no place else to go, many became victims of violence, disease, and crime. In order to survive, these young people sometimes committed crimes themselves. It seemed to be an unbreakable cycle that was repeated around the globe. The United Nations estimated there were 145 million abandoned children worldwide, meaning a lot of young lives were in need of assistance.

Neha wanted to do her part, so back home in Yardley, Pennsylvania, she took toys she no longer played with and sold them in a garage sale, putting the money to use to help others. But it wasn't long before she began thinking bigger: She wanted to break the cycle of poverty through education. Neha formed a nonprofit organization called Empower Orphans to help children around the world become self-sufficient.

Through her organization, which attracted donations and sponsorships from major corporations and foundations, Neha was able to set up computer labs, libraries, and sewing centers in India. With access to such resources, underprivileged children could learn skills that allowed them to find jobs as adults. Because of India's caste system, which separates people into different social classes, many people had never before had access to the kinds of resources that Empower Orphans provided.

One girl in India who received a sewing machine invited Neha to her home—a single room shared by five people. She told Neha that after she had

Neha poses next to some board games. The games are some of the 25,000 children that she has helped throu her organizati

learned to sew she could afford to give her family electricity. That allowed her to work at night and let her brother study to pass his electrician's exam. Both children added to the family's finances because of Neha's help.

Empower Orphans also offered healthcare resources and living necessities to children in need. Neha created an eye and dental clinic that provides are to more than 300 children. She also installed a well and water purification system. The well delivered clean drinking water for thousands of people.

014 Neha had raised more
$1.3 million to help
ren around the world.

The organization made an impact closer to Neha's home as well as throughout the state of Pennsylvania. The organization donated home furnishings, diapers, clothes, shoes, bicycles, and food to thousands of children.

By the time she was a senior in high school, Neha had won numerous awards for her efforts, including the prestigious World of Children Award and the Congressional Award Gold Medal. As the head of Empower Orphans she continued to look for opportunities to widen her influence, with plans to establish more libraries and computer labs at schools which served under represented children. She also wanted to double the number of children whose education costs were paid by her organization.

With plans to become a physician and serve underprivileged children around the world, Neha said the experiences she had and the people she met and helped were unforgettable. "They have shaped who I am," she said. "Empower Orphans has allowed me to find my voice and to speak out for those who cannot speak for themselves."

QUESTIONS TO THINK ABOUT

- Who was Mahatma Gandhi? If you don't know, do some research. What did he do? How did India change because of his efforts?
- Does your family have any traditions that help other people? What do you do?
- Have you ever helped or sold your own items at a garage sale? What did you do with the money you earned?
- What problems can occur when there is no electricity in your home?
- Have you ever felt discriminated against? What would you like to say to those who discriminated against you?

GRACE LI (2012)

"Every great change started with one person and one act."

Project: We Care Act

- Established in 2008
- Raised $70,000 for disaster relief
- Aided 14,000 people
- Provided leadership opportunities to 23,000 people in 17 countries
- Organized 400 activities, including workshops and philanthropy drives

Sichuan is the fifth largest province in China. Eighty million people live there. In 2008, an earthquake struck just 50 miles north of Chengdu, the capital of Sichuan. Tens of thousands of people died and millions more were left homeless.

Over 8,000 miles away near Pearland, Texas, 8th-grader Grace Li and her family watched the tragedy unfold on television. Grace's parents grew up in poor areas of China like the ones damaged by the Sichuan earthquake. Feeling a strong connection to the people affected, Grace decided that she needed to help.

Over the course of the next six years, Grace encouraged her family to raise funds and collect donations to help young victims of disasters around the world. Grace and her siblings went door-to-door to ask for donations. They organized silent auctions, which allowed people to bid on a variety of items and experiences (such as being guest host on a radio program). In the very first month she raised $4,500 and collected books and school supplies. She and her family travelled to Sichuan to deliver their donations directly to young schoolchildren affected by the earthquake.

Grace with her sister baking for Sandy Hook victims

Grace knew that while she had made a difference, it was just the start of much more she could do. She also knew that while raising money was good, it was not a long-term solution. Having met a lot of young people affected by disasters, Grace realized that when young people are given the opportunity, they are eager to serve, learn, and teach others. That realization became the basis for We Care Act, a nonprofit organization Grace founded to manage her charitable efforts.

By 2014 We Care Act had become a multinational organization with Grace as its chief executive officer (CEO). By connecting with individual students or schools in places that experienced natural disasters, We Care Act helped schoolchildren recover. The organization

Grace smiles knowing that she has helped to change the world.

perated programs throughout the world—workshops or children in China to learn English, a letter-writing campaign to boost the spirits of Japanese children affected by the earthquake and tsunami in 2011, donations of stuffed animals, clothing, food, and books for young victims of a typhoon in the Philippines.

From aiding the victims of natural disasters to running events to raise awareness about autism and child hunger, Grace and We Care Act sought to lift the spirits and improve the lives of children around the world. The organization even ran training programs to teach young people how they could have a positive impact on the lives of people both within and beyond their own communities.

After graduating from Glenda Dawson High School in Pearland, Grace received an academic scholarship from Duke University in Durham, North Carolina. Majoring in organic chemistry and considering a career in either medicine or law, she turned most of the day-to-day duties of running We Care Act over to her two younger siblings. However, she still made time for the organization when she could.

Though she was a winner of numerous awards for her service work, Grace didn't paper her dormitory room walls with evidence of her accomplishments. Instead, she taped a printout of an email she received from a 2nd-grader on the other side of the country,

Grace and her siblings packing aid supplies for the Philippines.

telling her that he chose her for his school's first ever Young Changemaker Award. For Grace, knowing that she had inspired the next generation of philanthropists was the best reward of all.

QUESTIONS TO THINK ABOUT
- Have you or someone you know ever experienced a natural disaster? What was lost?
- Research ideas for running a silent auction. What are some ideas for items you could sell?
- Have you ever gone door-to-door for a fundraiser? What was it for?
- Have you ever donated to a nonprofit organization?
- Do you think it is important to teach others how to help others? Why or why not?

CHARLES ORGBON III (2013)

"Find really good mentors."

Project: Greening Forward

- Established in 2008
- Built the largest youth-driven, youth-imagined national environmental nonprofit
- Raised $120,000 in five years
- Promoted youth-driven environmental action in 15 communities
- Involved 2,000 students and had an impact on 10,000 community members

As a 5th-grader in Dacula, Georgia, Charles Orgbon III attended a school that required students to take part in service learning. Noticing all the litter scattered around his school's campus, he decided his service would be to stay after school and help clean up the grounds.

Inspired by the experience, Charles joined with some other students to found an organization called the Earth Savers Club. They concentrated not only on the beautification of the school, but also the community around it.

But the Earth Savers Club was only the beginning for Charles. Wondering if he could get students at other schools interested in environmental issues too, he created Greening Forward, a website

Attendees at Charles' first International Young Environmentalist Youth Summit learning how to be "green."

that let kids discuss environmental issues and the impact on their lives and their communities.

From the beginning, Greening Forward was more than a website. It was a way for Charles to help his peers see that they had the power to improve their communities by improving the environment around them. He spent between 15 and 18 hours each week compiling more than 100 curriculum resources. He developed Greening Forward into a well-structured organization, and built relationships with corporations who could fund ideas developed by the website's users.

Greening Forward planned the first International Young Environmentalists Youth Summit, which brought together more than 100 young leaders for a three-day, two-night conference on environmental issues. Charles also helped begin days of service that encouraged students to plant trees and clean up rivers.

Charles and Greening Forward made a profound impact on environmental conditions in Georgia, while also teaching young people they have the power to change the world. Through the organization, volunteers built an outdoor classroom for a high school in Atlanta, Georgia. It sent young people to the Rio+20 Summit, the United Nations Conference on Sustainable Development in Rio de Janeiro, Brazil. Students involved with Greening Forward also monitored estuary health in South Carolina's low country, built composting bins n Aurora, Illinois, and recycled thousands of plastic products in Long Island, New York.

A 2014 graduate of Mill Creek High School in Hoschon, Georgia, Charles planned to continue his environmental work and his work as CEO of Greening Forward. Ideally, he said, the organization would continue to mentor student leaders and eventually be run by a full-time staff.

Until then, Charles—a frequent public speaker on environmental issues—planned to attend college in New England and follow the advice of one of the 20th century's most influential thinkers, Mahatma Gandhi, who said: "Live as if you were to die tomorrow. Learn as if you were to live forever."

Charles as a POCA winner sharing his infectious smile and attitude.

QUESTIONS TO THINK ABOUT

- What do you know about climate change or other environmental issues? What do you think should be done about climate change?
- Is your favorite animal endangered? Why is preserving endangered species important?
- Is litter a problem in your neighborhood? Why should people not litter?
- Can you do anything to make your life more "green"?
- Do you and your family recycle? Why or why not?
- What do you think Gandhi meant when he said, "Live as if you were to die tomorrow. Learn as if you were to live forever"?

CHRISTOPHER YAO (2013)

"Don't be afraid to stand up for what you believe in, even if you're standing alone."

Project: Kids Change the World

- Established in 2007
- Raised money for 70 cleft lip surgeries
- Attracted 19,000 volunteers and youth leaders
- Involved in 34 different countries
- Partnered with the Daos Children's Centre in Kenya

When Christopher Yao was in 6th grade, he was diagnosed with a class III malocclusion. That means Christopher's teeth and jaw were not lined up the way they were supposed to be. He had an underbite that, if left untreated, would have become worse until eventually he would not have been able to eat or speak properly.

Fortunately, with the help of a doctor, Christopher's jaw misalignment was corrected. Long since recovered from his experience, Christopher became curious about the fates of others with problems like his. Research soon revealed that worldwide one in every 700 hundred children are born with cleft lips and palates. A cleft means an opening, so children with cleft lips or palates have openings in their lips or the roofs of their mouths that didn't close during their bodies' development.

Christopher speaking at one of his many engagement to support his projec

Both problems can be solved with oral surgeries, but they are quite expensive, averaging between $5,000 and $10,000 each. Parents in poorer countries often can't afford to help their children who suffer from a cleft lip or palate. Many of those children are abandoned by their families and shunned by others.

Inspired by his grandfather, who had worked hard and made sacrifices to become a physician, Christopher wanted to help those children. Yet despite the fact that Christopher was motivated, a lot of the organizations he asked to help him didn't think a young boy could accomplish something so ambitious.

Christopher and other volunteers from Kids Change the World inspired children around the world to make an impact on their communities.

Then Christopher found and teamed up with Smile Train, an organization that provides free cleft surgeries to children around the world. He created a Read-a-Thon to raise the money needed to perform those surgeries. Christopher went to schools and libraries in his hometown of Jericho, New York, and encouraged kids to read more. He also asked them to get their family, friends, and neighbors to make a donation for every book or every page read. Christopher then provided prizes based on how much money they raised.

As a result of his efforts Christopher and the readers he inspired raised enough money to pay for over 0 surgeries around the world! The Power of Children Award that Christopher received funded eight surgeries. Seeing how much of an impact he had made in the lives of others, Christopher created Kids Change the World, which helps kids start and run their own fundraisers and programs worldwide. The organization helps raise money and provide start-up grants, website assistance, and free grassroots services.

Christopher said he created Kids Change the World because so many people had told him there was nothing he could do as a kid to help improve the world. He proved them wrong and he wanted to help other young people do the same. For his efforts on behalf of young philanthropists, he was selected as a 2014 Nickelodeon HALO Effect Honoree.

Including charitable work in everything that he does is very important to Christopher. A freshman at the University of Pennsylvania in Philadelphia, in 2014 he planned to major in biology and was interested in medicine and dentistry. He wanted to continue to help children with cleft lip and palate problems. At the same time he wanted to continue to be involved in community service projects because he found it so rewarding.

"I built Kids Change the World on the philosophy of empowering young people to make a difference in the lives of others," he said. "There is no limit to accomplishing the extraordinary."

QUESTIONS TO THINK ABOUT

- Have you ever had surgery on your mouth? What was it for? Do you know how much it cost?
- Have you ever volunteered for a cause? What did you do?
- How do you handle meeting someone who is physically different from you?
- Members of Christopher's family made him realize he wanted to help others. Who in your life inspires you to be a better person?

EDUCATORS

When you read the word *educators*, what comes to mind? The teachers in your school classrooms and hallways? The administrators, counselors, and coaches? Yes, all of them are educators—it's their job to teach their students both academic skills and life lessons.

But an educator could also be your best friend, brother, sister, cousin, or even the student you sit behind in algebra class can also be an educator. Broadly speaking, an educator is anyone who teaches you something useful, someone who expands your understanding of what it means to be alive. That certainly applies to the Power of Children Award recipients profiled in this section.

In addition to helping people in need, these individuals shined a light on problems that most other people were unaware even existed. For these youth, part of helping others was educating the general public about concerns, needs, and issues that were unrecognized and therefore lower priorities when it came to resources like funding, volunteer services, and publicity.

You've probably heard someone in your life say that knowledge is power. It's true. The more people know about a problem, the more likely they are to help solve it. The educators in this section set out to teach people about specific problems, with the goal of solving those problems by both working on the problems themselves and attracting public attention as they did so. They solicited donations. They convinced others to help them in their efforts. They made invisible problems visible.

None of us knows everything. The world is too complex, and people's needs are too numerous. Despite the fact that we are told we live in an information age, we remain uninformed about so much in our own communities, let alone elsewhere in the country or world. If we're lacking information, then we're also lacking knowledge. That's why we need educators. They inform the uninformed. They help us gain knowledge.

The young people profiled in this section earned the right to be called educators by teaching lessons in compassion, empathy, and dedication. And they taught in the best possible way—by example.

~ ~ ~

NIKIEIA (FITZPATRICK) JOHNSON (2005)

"Set your goals and reach them. There is no such thing as dreaming too big."

Project: Reading Club
- Established in 2002
- Served 25 children annually
- Improved reading skills and grades for all participants
- Encouraged the creation of a project in which teens could talk about issues they faced

If you've ever gotten so caught up in a book that you lost track of time or forgot where you were, then you know the joy of reading. But what if you couldn't do that because you couldn't read very well? Unfortunately, there are many kids for whom reading is a scary challenge rather than a pleasure. Nikieia Fitzpatrick recognized that problem in her community and set out to solve it.

As a member of the Boys and Girls Club in her hometown of Lake Station, Indiana, Nikieia Fitzpatrick recognized the value of education and positive role models. The Boys and Girls Club is an organization that helps young people become productive, caring, and responsible citizens. The clubs provide after-school programs. Through these programs, students have a safe and educational environment to go to outside of school.

Nikiea saw a way to fill a gap for the kids who came to the club. After seeing that many of the children she knew from the club were not reading at their grade levels, she created a Reading Club at the Boys and Girls Club. She knew that reading is a very important skill in life. Kids who read well also do better in school. They have better vocabularies and a better understanding of their assignments. In turn, better grades lead to better opportunities after graduation— college scholarships, jobs that pay well, a lifelong interest in reading and learning, and a deeper curiosity about other people, places, and events.

When Nikieia started the program with only five kids between the ages of 7 and 9, she realized that she had two problems to solve. The first was how to get more kids interested in reading. The second was how to keep their attention.

To solve those problems, Nikieia had to think creatively. She thought that if the topic was interesting, then kids would be more likely to read. She decided the children who were part of the Reading Club should be able to read whatever they wanted.

By getting participants actively involved in how they used their time, Nikieia made it more attractive to join the Reading Club. They had fun while building a love for reading. Soon more than 20 kids wanted to take part in the program.

Nikieia is the oldest of seven children and was the first in her family to earn a college degree.

Through her efforts Nikieia left a lasting mark on the Boys and Girls Club in Lake Station. As of 2014, the Reading Club was still inspiring young people to read. Though she didn't keep records of the number of students who were members of the club, she did know that many who participated in the club saw their classroom grades improve.

In addition to the Reading Club, Nikieia created a teen-centered program that connected adolescents with positive role models. Teens in the program could talk about choices they faced and get advice. They could talk about personal relationships, school, life, or their future plans.

When she won the Power of Children Award, Nikieia thought she wanted to be a pediatrician. It

Nikieia landed her dream job with a Boys and Girls Club in Arizona but still finds time for a little bit of golf.

didn't take her long to realize that her true passion was something different. Because of her work with the Boys and Girls Club, she wanted to educate young people

and provide them with positive role models. After graduating from Purdue University Calumet, where she received a bachelor's degree in human development and an associate's degree in early childhood development, Nikieia landed her dream job with another Boys and Girls Club in Peach Springs, Arizona.

While she focused on teaching young people about the value of positive role models, she became one herself. A three-time Youth of the Year Award winner at the Boys and Girls Club in Lake Station and a recipient of the Youth of the Year Award of Northwest Indiana, Nikieia was the first of her family to earn a college degree. The oldest of seven children, she showed her brothers and sisters that a college education is possible with hard work, perseverance, and making positive choices. She continues to encourage her family and the young people she works with to ignore any negative labels others may try to put on them and pursue their dreams.

From creating a reading club to working at her dream job, Nikieia was inspired to make great things happen for herself and others through her belief that there are no limits to what she or anyone else can achieve in life.

QUESTIONS TO THINK ABOUT
- What does it mean to be a positive role model? What qualities make someone a role model?
- Who are your role models? What do you admire about them? Are they positive role models?
- Who else in your family has gone to college or technical school or had an apprenticeship? Who were their role models?
- Do you participate in an after-school program? What is it? How does or did it affect you?
- What are your plans for the future? Who do you share your dreams with? What choices do you have to make to get the future you want?
- How can you help others succeed?

ABRAXAS SEGUNDO GARCIA (2005)

"When someone tells you that something can't be done and that you can't possibly change it, show them just how great you are."

roject: *Hola Bloomington*
- Established in 2005
- Provided technical support for *Hola Bloomington,* a radio show for Spanish-speaking listeners
- Helped increase the quality and visibility of audio programming
- Created a radio program logo
- Contributed to a sense of community and unity within the Spanish-speaking population

or many people, listening to the radio is an important part of their lives. Some listen to muc, others to talk shows, sports broadcasts, or news. ome listen in their cars, others in their kitchens or ffices. Some have clock radios set so their favorite ations wake them up in the morning. Others have mers set to turn their radios on when they come ome at night.

For Abraxas Segundo García, it didn't matter here people were listening. He just wanted them to sten because he believed radio was a means of overoming language and cultural differences.

Although he was born in the United States, braxas grew up in Mexico. When he moved to loomington, Indiana, to attend high school he was uent in Spanish, but knew little English. As he beame more comfortable speaking English, he started oking for something to do outside of school. He as staying with a family and his hosts suggested at he look for places where he could get involved the community. In a meeting with an advisor, he arned about a new hour-long radio show called *Hola loomington.* The show became one of many volunteer pportunities Abraxas took advantage of while he was high school.

In addition to learning a new language, another challenge Abraxas faced was cultural differences. The people of Mexico and the United States have different customs and laws. The purpose of *Hola Bloomington* was to help listeners overcome both the language and cultural barriers.

The program reached out to Spanish speakers, telling them about

Abraxas started his radio program to help people overcome language and cultural differences.

events happening in and around Bloomington and nearby communities. It also informed them about local, state, and federal laws and policies that could affect them. It was a lifeline for listeners as they learned a new language and adapted to a new culture. It was also a source of entertainment.

Abraxas was the youngest person working on the show. However, his age did not stop him from making significant contributions. He worked behind the scenes operating the soundboard and microphones during air time. He also collaborated with others on the scripts used for the show. He became an essential part of the show's volunteer production staff.

Throughout high school Abraxas contributed as much time, energy, and effort as he could to *Hola Bloomington*. The show became a beacon for the Spanish-speaking population and a bridge between its members and their English-speaking neighbors.

Abraxas eventually had to leave the show when he enrolled at Indiana University. A musician and composer, he worked on degrees in enthnomusicology, anthropology, and sociology. But his busy schedule meant that Abraxas did not have as much time as he would have liked for *Hola Bloomington*. When he couldn't help out he made sure that he found other talented people who could. He also helped create the first Hispanic radio talk show while at IU.

The impact of *Hola Bloomington*, which was still going strong nine years after its 2005 debut, was immeasurable. It helped countless people learn about the English language and American culture. As *Hola Bloomington* got more popular, listeners started reaching out to the show for advice, fun, and friendship. The show became the go-to place for everyone in the Spanish-speaking community. It let them know about social gatherings. It provided news and presented topics of interest to IU students and the Bloomington community.

Abraxas eventually left Bloomington to study music composition at Centro Morelense de las Artes del Estado de Morelos in Cuernavaca, Mexico. In addition to writing and performing music, he began writing articles for scholarly publications on such topics as how universities view the effects of laws on society. He also began researching the Maya people of the Yucatán Peninsula, whose ancestors created the Maya Empire, which flourished throughout the region from 1800 BCE to 900 CE. His work with the Maya, which focused on the music and culture, led to the creation of a TV soap opera aimed at Mayans and performed in their language.

Abraxas said that the most important thing he learned from his experience with *Hola Bloomington* was the power of believing in himself. He learned that by believing in himself and what he was doing, he was able to keep going in times when it would have been easy to quit.

QUESTIONS TO THINK ABOUT

- Have you ever wanted to communicate with someone but couldn't due to a language barrier? What did you do?
- Do you listen to the radio? If you do, do you listen to music? Sports? News? Talk shows?
- Are you a musician? Do you sing or play an instrument? What have you learned from the experience? How can you share that?
- Do you know any other languages? Do you want to learn more? How did you learn your first language? How can learning another language teach you about another culture?
- How can playing music can be philanthropic?

SHELBY MITCHELL (2006)

"Move on from adversity and help other people."

Project: Sheltering Wings
- Mentored children who experienced domestic violence
- Organized fund-raisers to raise money for and awareness about domestic violence

There are things that happen in life that are hard to imagine unless you've experienced them. Then they're hard to forget. For Shelby Mitchell, one of those unimaginable things happened on April 13, 2004, and changed her life forever.

Shelby, her three sisters and two brothers started that Tuesday like they did any other weekday. Those who were old enough got ready for school and left. The youngest brother stayed home.

When Shelby and her sisters got home from school, their house was surrounded by police cars, fire trucks, ambulances, and helicopters. Their father stood in the driveway of their home, holding their 2-year-old brother in his arms. When they asked him what happened, he didn't say anything.

Not knowing what to do, Shelby and her siblings went to a neighbor's house. Several hours later, they heard the worst news a child could hear. Their father had shot their mother to death, making the Mitchells six of the more than 3 million children who experience domestic violence in the United States every year.

Shelby's mother, Cindy, was loved by everyone she met, and no one understood how such a thing could have happened. With their father in police custody, Shelby and her siblings stayed with family members as they tried to piece their lives back together. Shelby knew that her mother would have wanted them to move on and help other people.

Shelby then began volunteering with an organization called Sheltering Wings, in Danville, Indiana. Sheltering Wings provides emergency housing for victims of domestic violence. The organization also runs a 24-hour crisis phone line and community outreach programs, and provides children and adults with supportive programs. Children who have experienced domestic abuse have access to age-appropriate classes, support groups, and crisis intervention services.

Going to the shelter and talking with kids always made Shelby's day a little bit better.

Shelby became a mentor at Sheltering Wings. She met with children and talked with them about what they were thinking and feeling. The children knew that Shelby also understood what they were going through since she had experienced the worst.

Shelby was a natural role model for the children who needed a safe space. Her work as a mentor was also helpful to Shelby as she tried to heal herself. Even when she had a tough day, going to the shelter and talking with the kids always made her day just a little bit better.

Shelby also helped with mentoring and running fund-raisers for the organization. She was a model for the fashion show called Dazzling Designs and helped plan a 10-mile walk/run. Both fund-raisers collected money to provide better living at the shelter.

When Shelby won the Power of Children Award, she planned on having a career in elementary education or child development. Her work with Sheltering Wings encouraged her to look for ways to help children. She plans to do what she can to make sure that no one goes through what her mother an her siblings went through.

QUESTIONS TO THINK ABOUT

- Have you ever mentored other people? What did you talk about?
- Are there organizations in your area that help families who have experienced domestic violence? What do those organizations do? Do they need volunteer help or donated supplies?
- How do you think you can help others who have experienced very bad situations in their lives? What do you think they may need beyond supplies?
- Do you know what to do if you or anyone you know experiences violence at home?
- Do you know what a crisis hotline is? How can you find more information on what they do?

BRITTANY OLIVER (2007)

*"Choosing a cause and committing to it is the most important step.
Then you just continue working toward what you believe."*

Project: Reading Teams
- Active 2005–2008
- Hundreds of books distributed to children
- 20 active reading teams involving 80 volunteers
- 500 hours contributed by volunteers

People all over the world struggle with so many problems that it's easy to feel there's nothing one person can do to make a difference. Brittany Oliver didn't believe that. The citizens of Lafayette, Indiana, realized how right she was when Brittany developed a reading program that became the talk of the town.

Reading is something that many children struggle to master. Not every child likes to read, especially when told what to read or assigned to read something that's too difficult. When that happens, those children may do poorly on tests and in school. With 66 percent of 8th-graders reading below their grade level, it was clear to Brittany that there was a need for help outside of the classroom.

In 2005, she launched her project called Reading Teams. It began at a conference where Brittany joined with others to help young children learn that reading can be fun, not just something that a teacher or a parent makes them do.

Brittany studied in Spain and has a degree in chemistry.

She arranged for volunteers to read to groups of children at the local YMCA. Brittany soon realized the children needed more structure and the program needed more volunteers. She paired volunteers so if one was sick or couldn't make it on a particular day, the other one could take over. If both of them came, they could provide more one-on-one time with students. This allowed students to get the help they needed. It also made it easier on the volunteers.

Eventually, Brittany contacted daycare centers and after-school programs. She asked them if they would like volunteers to come in and read. Gradually she arranged a schedule, and more and more volunteers gave their time.

Soon, she started collecting books, even using her Power of Children Award grant to buy more. Students in the program were given books to take home, an

Brittany demonstrates her many talents.

important benefit since 42 percent of American children grow up in homes where there are no books. Once the community and the media discovered what Brittany was doing, she became known as "the girl with the reading program."

When Brittany graduated from high school, she could not continue the program. But she didn't lose her passion for community service. After earning her degree in chemistry at Purdue University in West Lafayette, Indiana, Brittany enrolled in Purdue's pharmacy program to earn a doctorate. A mentor in the Women in Science program at Purdue, she helped organize health fairs for the local community. She also made time to read to students at the Purdue Village Preschool, and got involved with organizations like the Boys and Girls Club. Believing that service is an important part of life, she focused her efforts on empowering others to help themselves.

Brittany learned how to put others in positions to help people in need, a skill that was helpful when she chaired the community projects committee for the Academy of Student Pharmacists. She figured out the best way to get volunteers working together to make the biggest impact. She also learned that most people are willing to help when asked.

While Brittany committed a lot of time to the Reading Teams program, she recognized that its success came from her volunteers. She got them involved because she was not afraid to commit to a cause she cared about or to ask others for help.

QUESTIONS TO THINK ABOUT
- Why is reading important?
- Do you like reading? If you do, who inspired you to read? If you don't, why not?
- What is your favorite book? What would you be like if you never read it?
- What can you do to help others read? Who can you ask to help you help others?
- How would your daily life be different if you did not know how to read?

CARAH AUSTIN (2009)

"Never let your age or position in life determine the possibilities of what you can accomplish!"

Project: Find a Book a Home Foundation/History Makers of the Future

Established in 2004/2007

Created seven new hospital libraries for pediatric and adult patients

Provided 800 students with free historical and educational trips

Distributed 900,000 books to schools, senior centers, hospitals, disaster relief agencies, and agencies in the Cherokee Nation

Donated books and stuffed animals to children participating through other organizations' programs

The American philosopher George Santayana once wrote: "Those who cannot remember the past are condemned to repeat it." Carah Austin is doing her best to make sure Indiana students learn a lot from (and about) the past.

Carah's passion started at a book fair. She overheard another girl ask her family for a book, but they could not afford it. Carah, who was 11 at the time, wondered how a kid like her could get books to people who could not afford them.

On that day, Carah's mission to put books in every home began. She established the Find a Book a Home Foundation. She started small by having donation tables available at her school. She spent her own allowance on prizes to encourage donations. The books she received were then given to various organizations, including disaster relief programs. Victims of Hurricane Katrina in 2005 and the 2008 floods in Indiana had access to books.

One of Carah's biggest challenges was convincing adults that a young person could manage large projects. But she had a vision. She kept looking for ways to get books.

Her donation tables became grander and the stacks of books they attracted grew taller. Because she had so many books, Carah created her first library in a hospital in 2007. It was in the pediatric ward at King's Daughters' Hospital in Madison, Indiana. She credited the hospital with saving her life when she contracted spinal meningitis, an inflammation of the brain and spinal cord protective membranes, a few years earlier. Based on the success of the pediatric ward library, she created multiple libraries for patients throughout the hospital.

While at a book fair, Carah overheard a family mention they could not afford to buy a book.

While it was rewarding to give away thousands of books, Carah looked for more hands-on ways to help children learn. Through her foundation she created the History Makers of the Future program, which led to her Power of Children Award. In 2007, the first year of the program, donors provided funding to pay for 120 children to take a trip to Madison. On the banks of the Ohio River, the southern Indiana town is one of the largest National Historic Landmark Districts in the United States. Each summer since, Carah has organized a similar trip and provided an educational experience to hundreds of 4th-graders in Indiana.

After graduating from high school Carah, whose projects earned her a Gold Medal Congressional Award, enrolled in Butler University in Indianapolis.

Carah helped youths in many places to become involved in her projects.

With a major in biology and minors in chemistry and health care management, she divided her time between her studies and her philanthropic work. After graduating from Butler she planned on attending medical school to become a gastrointestinal surgeon, fixing patients' problems with their stomachs and intestines.

In the meantime, she headed Butler's chapter of Alpha Phi Omega, a national service fraternity that trains its members for leadership through service. She also volunteered at free medical clinics, a step toward her professional goal of bringing medical care to disadvantaged children and the homeless.

According to Carah, a service project is like a 5,000-piece jigsaw puzzle. At the beginning, the pieces are scattered and putting them together seems impossible. But you start with one piece here and another there, and eventually a picture develops. Before long, something big has been created, one small piece at a time.

QUESTIONS TO THINK ABOUT

- What is your favorite subject in school? What could get others interested in that subject?
- Do you know much about the state you live in? Do some research about historic figures or events in your state.
- Is there a historical society, library, or book club in your neighborhood that needs volunteers?
- Have you ever thought about creating your own club or group to explore something you are interested in?
- Have you ever read a memoir or an interesting historical story? What did you learn?

AMBER KRIECH (2009)

*"You don't have to do something big and extravagant to make a difference;
in fact, the small things are just as important."*

Project: Eager Reader Reading Program
Established in 2008
Created media center and library
Recruited 30 volunteers, ages 9 to 80, who contributed 72 hours
Built 6 bookcases and obtained more than 2,000 books
Served more than 100 students per year

What does carpentry have to do with reading books? Just ask Amber Kriech.

Her mother used to be a teacher in a low-income, high-crime area of Indianapolis. When she passed away, Amber's family wanted to honor her by helping others. They brought backpacks filled with school supplies to the school where her mother taught and there students often lacked the supplies they needed to succeed in the classroom. Without the tools they needed in school or at home, they couldn't take notes or complete their homework. Amber and her family recognized that not having these materials was having a negative effect on the students.

Many of the students who attended the school where her mother taught also went to the East Tenth United Methodist Children and Youth Center in Indianapolis. Amber discovered that many of the youngsters who visited the center had no access to educational items outside of school, so she bought supplies from the local Goodwill Store and donated them. When she saw what an impact her gift had on the children at the center, Amber was determined to do more. She collected art supplies and bought six new easels to encourage students' creativity.

But Amber knew that school supplies could only do so much. She wanted to share her love of reading, especially with the students who were not doing well in school. They needed a place designed to encourage them to read.

Amber decided to build a library.

She purchased the supplies she needed and built six bookcases. She scoured secondhand shops and

Amber received a POCA scholarship to attend IUPUI.

online outlets for gently used books and other items like tables, benches, and beanbag chairs. She recruited volunteers of all ages to help her. When she was done, the students who came to East Tenth had a new library and media center, a safe and inviting place they could visit before and after school to inspire them. The entire project, which might have cost $3,500 if Amber bought everything new, actually cost only $305 thanks to her careful shopping and donated items.

After creating the library at East Tenth, she set up the Eager Reader Reading Program. Students who completed the program were awarded certificates and prizes. Amber also created Rolling Libraries 4 Kids, a program that, by 2014, had donated over 10,500 books to after-school programs. Two thousand disadvantaged youths had gained access to books after school because of Amber.

Amber used her Power of Children grant to spread her philanthropic spirit further. Learning that one out of every three people who are homeless is under the age of 18, she renovated an unfinished attic for a local homeless outreach organization. What was once a storage space became a center with a meeting room for one-on-one counseling, a chapel, a training room, and an inspirational library.

After graduating from Carmel High School in Carmel, Indiana, Amber—a recipient of the Indiana Governor's Service Award—remained committed to making life better in her community. As a student at Indiana University-Purdue University Indianapolis majoring in organizational leadership and supervision, she used what she learned to inspire others to get involved.

"I remember being a 14-year-old and feeling so overwhelmed and discouraged about halfway through my library project," she recalled. "Those feelings are

Amber did more than just raise mon

normal. Overcoming difficulties and learning fror your experiences is how you grow and gain the conf dence to go forward to accomplish your goals."

QUESTIONS TO THINK ABOUT
- What do you do after school each day? Do you volunteer? If so, why? If not, why not?
- What skills do you have that could help people in need?
- Have you ever felt overwhelmed by a project? What did you do to overcome your challenges? Did anyone help you?
- Do you have a special place where you like to spend your free time?

DALE PEDZINSKI (2009)

"K.I.S.S. — Keep It Simple Stupid.
This one phrase has kept me from over-thinking and over-complicating tasks."

Project: Thumb Drives for the Homeless
Established in 2009
Wrote a United Way grant and received $4,300 for the project
Helped seven people find permanent work
Gave thumb drives for storing résumés to people who were homeless

Dale raised money to give thumb drives to people who were homeless to store their important information like resumés.

Imagine the following scenario. You have no job and you just lost your house because you couldn't make your monthly payment. Now you spend your nights at a local homeless shelter. In order to get back on your feet, you try to find another job. You have a few interviews in the next week. How do you prepare?

Dale Pedzinski learned that many homeless residents in Indianapolis lacked the computer skills they needed to conduct a successful job search. To help them, he started a program at Horizon House, a local shelter. The program was aimed at teaching homeless individuals the skills they needed to find jobs and become financially independent.

When Dale began his twice-monthly program, only three people showed up. But they learned valuable skills and enjoyed it so much that they told others. Soon Dale had a packed classroom.

Initially he taught skills like writing cover letters and résumés, but his students pointed out that they needed to learn more. Dale added other lessons on using computer programs such as Excel and PowerPoint. He also taught how to search job sites on the web and how to use email to apply for jobs and maintain contact with employment agencies and employers.

Regrettably, the homeless shelter did not have up-to-date computers or even a printer, so Dale's students could not print out their résumés. Dale realized it would be difficult for homeless people to carry copies of their new résumés with them anyway. Then he learned he could write a grant application to the social services agency United Way to raise the money he needed to solve that problem.

Dale called his plan Thumb Drives for the Homeless. His grant was approved and with the $4,300 he received he bought 100 thumb drives. The drives allowed his students to carry their résumés with them. When job opportunities came up, they could email copies of their résumé to potential employers or print them off at a library and deliver them in person.

Dale also created a computer manual for students attending his classes. He passed out training certificates to everyone who did well. The $2,000 grant he received as a Power of Children Awards recipient allowed him to purchase more thumb drives. He also reserved some of the money to pay for cupcakes to celebrate each time someone got a job.

In 2015, Dale married his college sweetheart.

After graduating from Cathedral High School i Indianapolis, Dale attended Rose-Hulman Institut of Technology in Terre Haute, Indiana. After com pleting his degree in software engineering in 201! he went to work as a software developer for a com pany in Maryland. Though Dale wasn't able to con tinue his work with the homeless shelter once h began college, he continued his charitable work b organizing an annual food drive in Terre Haute an assisting with a project that raised funds for floo victims.

Horizon House continued to operate the pro gram Dale created. And his computer manual a lowed new students to continue gaining the skil they needed to improve their personal and profes sional lives.

QUESTIONS TO THINK ABOUT

- What do you know that you could teach others?
- Why do you think people become homeless? List a few reasons and talk to a friend or family member to get additional ideas.
- What kinds of problems could not having a computer at home cause?
- Have you ever tried to start something but it was not successful right away? Did you stick with it, change it, or stop doing it? Why?

NATE OSBORNE (2011)

"When you have a team of people it is so much easier to move a project forward, and a group's enthusiasm and excitement are infectious and can help the project grow."

Project: Ken-ya Help Us?
- Established in 2008
- Raised $130,000
- Supported 128 orphaned and vulnerable children through high school in Kenya
- 200 volunteers helped at an annual carnival
- 12 adult mentors and 26 youth leaders participated

Wildebeests, rhinos, elephants, hippos, lions— The Republic of Kenya in eastern Africa is full of wildlife. What it does not have are many jobs that provide its citizens with a living wage. According to the Central Intelligence Agency's World Factbook, in 2012 more than 43% of Kenyans, or nearly 20 million people, lived in poverty. Lack of money makes it harder for Kenyan children to get an education, which means fewer of them go to college. And that means lower-wage jobs, leading to a continuing cycle of poverty.

Nate Osborne, a freshman at Brebeuf Jesuit Preparatory School in Indianapolis, Indiana, was inspired to help others by his mother, who encouraged him to do something beyond himself. He learned that many orphaned and vulnerable children were unable to get an education in Kenya. He decided to do something about it.

Nate founded the Ken-ya Help Us? project. Its first fund-raiser on behalf of Kenyan children was a garage sale. From that small beginning came a student-led interfaith organization that held an annual community-wide carnival. In its first three years the Ken-ya Help Us? Carnival raised $65,000. That was enough money to support 25 high school students in western Kenya for one year.

Ken-ya Help Us? had both global and local impacts. Globally, it helped dozens of orphans and underprivileged children in Kenya afford to go to school. One of the directors of the project in Kenya said that student leaders were stepping forward. Because of Nate and his volunteers, other students were being inspired to act. Not only were they getting an education, they were helping themselves and others.

Locally, Ken-ya Help Us? taught people in Indianapolis about the effects of global poverty on real people and showed them there was something they could do to combat it. It also gave Nate and other students opportunities to be leaders. They were trained to become good leaders, and they ran projects such as the carnival, which gave them actual leadership experience. After they graduated from high school, they were able to draw on what they learned from their experiences. Many went to work for corporations and nonprofits, or founded organizations of their own.

In 2011 Nate and a small group of other Ken-ya Help Us? volunteers went to Kenya to meet some of the students the organization had helped. It was a powerful reminder of why they were doing what they

Nate was a freshman in high school when he was inspired to help others.

were doing, Nate said. It was also a way to bridge the distance between two countries and build understanding between two cultures.

As of 2014 Ken-ya Help Us? was still active, having merged with Global Interfaith Partnership to better serve the children in Kenya. However, by that point Nate had stepped down as the organization's director, leaving it to other student leaders to carry on its mission. A sophomore at Boston College in Chestnut Hill, Massachusetts, he was studying philosophy and working on behalf of such issues as climate change and social justice.

For Nate, his work with Ken-ya Help Us? was just the beginning of what he considered a lifelong

Nate and his friend Tobias from Kenya.

Several friends participated in a fundraiser with Na[...] and they met Indianapolis Mayor Greg Balla[...]

quest for ways to have a positive impact on the world Through new experiences and contact with a variety of people, he intended to continue learning and putting his knowledge to use on behalf of others.

QUESTIONS TO THINK ABOUT

- How has your life changed because of education? How would your life be different without it?
- What goals do you have for yourself that you set because of what you learned?
- Have you ever been a leader? For what type of organization, group, or project? If not, would you like to be one? What would you like to lead?
- Can you be a leader without a title? Why or why not?
- What types of skills does a leader need? What's the difference between a good leader and a bad one?
- How familiar are you with issues in other countries such as Kenya? What do you know and what more can you find out?

SARAH WOOD (2012)

"Start addressing a bigger issue in your classroom, at your youth group, or in other smaller settings. The efforts will only grow from there."

Project: Depression Awareness
- Established in 2010
- Reached out to 3,500 students, teachers, and parents
- Awarded $1,000 grant to train staff at two middle schools
- Trained 30 staff members in a suicide prevention program
- Raised funds for the first crisis texting line in the state of Indiana

Taking steps toward good health is important to living a good life. Health professionals encourage us to exercise, eat well, and have regular checkups. But good health is more than just physical. We also have to take care of our mental health. Stress and anxiety can cause us to feel as miserable as if we were physically sick. In the same way that we can go to a doctor to treat our physical illnesses, we also can go to one to get mentally healthy.

However, a lot of people have the attitude that mental health is something each of us should be able to deal with on our own. They believe that a mental issue can be corrected merely by thinking differently.

But mental health problems can be caused by things outside of our control. Just as we cannot simply decide not to get a cold or cancer, we cannot decide not to have a mental illness. But because of the attitude that "it's all in your head," many people postpone seeing a doctor, hoping they can solve their problems on their own. Others avoid asking for help because they fear being teased or bullied.

Middle school is an especially difficult time to stay mentally healthy. As bodies change, emotions run high. Longstanding friendships fall apart. Social circles emerge, leaving some people feeling unwanted or invisible. Sarah Wood experienced some of those issues firsthand. She struggled with depression, self-injury, and thoughts of suicide.

Sarah fortunately had the support of a friend who encouraged her to talk with an adult about her struggles. She later said doing that saved her life. As Sarah recovered, she realized how many other kids her age had the same struggles she did. To address the issue, she developed Depression Awareness as a means of helping others learn about and cope with mental health issues.

When she was a freshman at Lawrence North High School in Indianapolis, Sarah set out to raise awareness on self-injury and suicide within middle schools. She wanted to teach students and teachers that recovery was possible and show them how to get help.

Sarah wanted to present her story to health classes in middle schools. But first she had to convince principals, counselors, and administrators from the school district's central office of the value of changing the perception of

Sarah taught middle-school students that recovery from depression was possible.

mental illness. Many of them were afraid to bring up such a serious issue with middle school students, believing that they couldn't handle it.

But Sarah convinced the skeptics and eventually was allowed to meet with 12 middle school health classes. She shared her story and produced a video series to reach more students. Some of her peers also shared their stories related to mental health in the video. She wanted to highlight this message for students: reach out, get help, there is hope.

Sarah realized from her interactions with students that many were curious about the symptoms of depression. She also was gratified that because of her

Sarah's collage was both soothing and uplifting.

talks, at least 19 students reached out to school counselors for help. Because depression is such a serious mental health issue, Sarah felt she would have succeeded if even one student had sought help.

After graduation, Sarah began pursuing degrees in psychology and Spanish at Indiana University in Bloomington. With plans to become a counselor, she continued her involvement with mental health awareness by working with such organizations as Mental Health America and Crimson CORPS, an awareness and training group. She hoped to expand Depression Awareness by training school nurses and producing more informational videos.

QUESTIONS TO THINK ABOUT

- Does it matter how many people you help through philanthropy, or does it just matter that you are helping people? Explain your answer.
- Have you ever been sad or depressed? How did you feel and how did it affect your daily life? Did you go to anyone for help?
- What would you do if a friend of yours seemed depressed or told you he or she was thinking of self-harm?
- How would you talk to a principal, guidance counselor, or another adult in order to get them to help you with a project you believe in?

MADELINE CUMBEY (2013)

"Not giving up is the difference between those who accomplish great things and those who don't."

Project: SMART2bfit

Established in 2010

Engaged 1,000 people in healthy activities

Provided organic food to 150 people

Produced 1,500 pounds of food for food banks

Raised $4,700

Built a water catchment tank for 281 schoolchildren in Kenya

When Madeline Cumbey was only 2 years old, she was diagnosed with high cholesterol. While human beings need high-density lipoprotein (HDL) cholesterol (sometimes called "good" cholesterol) to build healthy cells, its opposite low-density lipoprotein (LDL) cholesterol (sometimes called "bad"

Madeline's project taught kids how to grow fresh food and provide it to others in need.

cholesterol) can cause health problems. People can help maintain a good balance in their bodies by eating right and exercising.

So, Madeline learned at a young age the importance of eating healthy food. When she began volunteering at a food pantry in Fort Wayne, Indiana, at age 9, she noticed there was not very much fresh food available. Fresh food is often healthier than processed food, but it is usually more expensive.

Madeline's experience with her own health and her family's history of heart disease, stroke, and cancer led her to establish SMART2bfit (pronounced smart-to-be-fit). SMART stands for Service, Multipurpose, Activity, Real hope, and Teaching. She wanted to fight issues like hunger, thirst, and childhood obesity by growing fresh food and encouraging people to exercise. She thought that if kids could work together on such projects, the next generation would be a healthier one.

Madeline's project had three parts to it. SMART2bfit clubs promoted healthy habits by teaching kids how to cook healthier and how to be more active. SMART2bfit gardens gave kids the opportunity to learn how to grow food and also provided fresh produce for people in need. SMART2bfit walks raised awareness about the lack of access to safe, adequate water supplies, a problem that affects more than a billion people around the world. SMART2bfit also raised money to build wells in places such as Kenya and South Sudan, directly helping solve that very problem. The walks also gave people chances to get outside and be active.

Madeline used her Power of Children Award grant to create and maintain a website devoted to SMART2bfit. It also allowed supporters to donate to its cause. From the beginning Madeline and her younger brother Carter served as ambassadors for healthy living. As a 7th-grader in Oswego, Illinois, in 2014, she was invited to do a presentation about SMART2bfit at the 25th Annual Monumental Service Learning Conference in Washington, D.C., where she also received the annual Youth Leadership for

Service-Learning Excellence Award. While there she had the opportunity to tell her story to members of the U.S. Congress, and talked about the importance of service learning.

She used the extra grant money left after she created her website to create the fifth SMART kid community garden, in a town in Missouri. She hoped communities across the country would create additional SMART gardens, and she credited the Power of Children gallery at The Children's Museum of Indianapolis for inspiring her to continue her efforts to improve the diets and health of people around the world.

But she never forgot how SMART2bfit got started—with something that was important to her, which motivated her to do what she felt was right. "Know that you have power just being who you are," she said when asked what she would tell others considering service projects of their own. "Be yourself, tell your story, no one else can be you."

Another part of Madeline's campaign was to create Sm Gardens across the coun

QUESTIONS TO THINK ABOUT

- Is your favorite food healthy or unhealthy?
- What is your favorite way to stay active? Can you get others involved with this activity?
- What games can you play that are also exercise? How much exercise are we supposed to get each day? Check out some resources and programs that encourage healthy lifestyles.
- How can you be healthier with your daily food choices?
- What is a water catchment tank? Why is it useful?

MARIA KELLER (2013)

"Helping out in any way you can really makes a huge difference."

Project: Read Indeed
- Established in 2008
- Distributed 1,100,000 books
- Collected $50,000 in funds to help ship books
- Worked with 250 different organizations that serve children and teens
- Affected the lives of 500,000 children

Maria Keller had always loved books, and she read a lot of them. When she found out that some kids didn't read simply because they didn't have any books, she set out to change that.

Maria's goal was simple. She wanted to collect 1 million books by the time she was 18 years old. Because she was 8 at the time, that meant she had to collect 100,000 books every year for 10 years, an ambitious goal for anyone of any age.

Within five years of beginning her project, Maria surpassed her 10-year goal to collect 1 million books.

Maria spent 10 to 15 hours a week organizing books.

To help her get a book into every home in Plymouth, Minnesota, where she lived, she established a nonprofit organization called Read Indeed. Its mission was to make sure that every child who needed books got them. The organization adopted the slogan: "Making the world a better place, one book at a time."

From the time Read Indeed was founded in 2008, Maria spent between 10 and 15 hours a week organizing book drives, and then counting, sorting, and packing all the books the drives collected. She created a website that allowed people to easily volunteer and donate their own books. Schools, hospitals, homeless shelters, and other institutions serving children around the world could use the website to coordinate picking up books from Maria's warehouse to distribute.

Within five years of starting her project Maria had surpassed her 1 million book mark, with donations coming to her from around the country. She collected about 600 books a day between 2008 and 2013. She used the Power of Children Award grant she received to buy new books for young people in need.

Read Indeed received a tremendous amount of support from across the United States. As a winner of the prestigious Jefferson Award for public service, and named an Everyday Young Hero by Youth Service America, Maria inspired many people to create their own book drives in order to get books to children and teens who had no other access to them.

In addition to believing that everyone should have books, Maria recognized the value to people of volunteering in their communities. Whenever she had the chance, Maria accepted invitations to speak about her experiences as a way to encourage people to become volunteers and make significant contributions to their local communities.

QUESTIONS TO THINK ABOUT

- Many young people have trouble reading but are afraid to ask for help. Do you feel this way or know someone who does? How could you help them?
- Has anyone ever read to you? What effect did that have on you?
- What could you do to help a young person read better?
- Do you write your own stories? What are they about?

MATTHEW KAPLAN (2014)

"Community service is like planting seeds of compassion. Seeds may be tiny things, but they take root and grow, branching out in ways that you can't imagine."

Project: Be ONE Project

- Established in 2010
- 1,800 students have participated in three states
- Provided outreach programming to raise awareness about bullying
- Partnered with local suicide hotline
- Featured on Radio Disney Music Awards

Every school has at least one bully roaming the hallways. Maybe it's someone who pushes people around, shoves them into lockers, or knocks them down. Maybe it's someone who treats people badly, calls them names, or tells lies about them. Or maybe it's someone who uses the anonymity of social media to make fun of or harass others.

Online bullying—known as cyberbullying—is no less harmful, disturbing, or frightening to its victims than physical bullying. So when Matthew Kaplan's younger brother Josh became a target of cyberbullying, Matthew did what any older brother would—he stepped in to stop it. But instead of fighting his brother's battles or bullying the bullies, Matthew set out to end bullying altogether.

By doing so, Matthew became part of a nationwide effort by local and state governments, community organizations, and school systems to end bullying. While those efforts were admirable, Matthew wanted to find a way to confront and defeat the bullying problem more quickly. Realizing that a lot of anti-bullying projects were aimed at high school students, Matthew knew that children start bullying others, including his brother, earlier than that.

That was the basis for Matthew's Be ONE Project. ONE stands for "Open to New Experiences." Initially, Matthew just wanted to make a difference at his middle school, where he was an 8th-grader. His project became so successful, though, that it became part of his school's mandatory curriculum. Soon Matthew had a waiting list of schools wanting him to help them tackle the issue of bullying.

However, for Matthew, the success of his project never depended on how many schools signed up to participate. Instead, it was how the Be ONE Project affected the lives of students.

By way of an example, Matthew recalled the day he had spoken at one school. At the end

Matthew believes that everyone should be open to new experiences.

of the program, a student stepped up to the microphone and shared that he had had trouble making friends since Kindergarten. He hoped that things would change after the program and that his peers would stop making fun of him.

The next six students who came up to the microphone apologized for bullying their classmate. When Matthew checked in with the students' teacher later, he found that the bullying had ended and the student who had been its target was finally happy in school. Having received the Power of Children Award, Matthew continued looking for opportunities to expand the Be ONE Project. Ideally, he wanted to expand nationwide and to develop a "curriculum in a box" so that schools could use the program easily. He planned to use the Power of Children Award grant to help reach the large list of schools on his waiting list.

As he continued to develop the Be ONE Project, Matthew also looked to the future and how he might continue to make a difference in the lives of others. As he applied to various colleges, he looked for ones that would give him a chance to pursue a career in social advocacy through majors such as public policy or nonprofit management. Eventually, he hoped to get a master's degree in public policy and a law degree.

Remembering how his project began, Matthew said, "I had no special knowledge or particular skills when I started the Be ONE Project. I just saw a problem that I thought I might be able to solve. I had an

Matthew wants to end bullying altogether by helping students to understand the consequences.

idea, and I had the courage and conviction to run with it." That's what the Power of Children Awards honor.

QUESTIONS TO THINK ABOUT
- Have you ever been bullied? Do you know someone who has? How did you (or that person) deal with it?
- Have you ever bullied someone? Why? Do you know someone else who has bullied others?
- What do you think makes one person bully another?
- How can a bully change his/her behavior?
- How can someone who's being bullied change what's going on?
- If you're being bullied, do you know someone—a parent, teacher, counselor, friend—to whom you can talk about the problem? Speak up. Bullying often exists because victims refuse to say anything.

HELPERS

Have you ever seen someone in trouble and wanted to help? Maybe it was a family member who was sick, a friend who was struggling with a personal problem, or a stranger without bus fare or lunch money. Maybe it was a military veteran in a wheelchair trying to cross a busy street, an elderly neighbor with an armful of groceries, a child lost at the mall. Or maybe it was a man asleep in a cardboard box, a student without a pencil or a coat, or a town destroyed by a tornado.

Big or small, a problem is a problem and you just might have the solution. Or at least you want to help. Welcome to the human race. Most of us wish we could do something for people who are suffering. Some of us do. The ones who do are helpers.

Helpers recognize that aid comes in all sizes. Just because you're young doesn't mean you can't do anything. Just because you don't have the time, money, or experience to solve a problem all by yourself doesn't mean you can't contribute to its solution. And just because a problem may seem small in comparison to others that get more attention doesn't make it any less important to the people it affects.

Sometimes helpers are the first to respond to a need, and sometimes they're not. Sometimes they're on their own, and sometimes they're part of a bigger effort. Sometimes they do what they set out to do and move on to other challenges, and sometimes they form organizations dedicated to a specific cause and continue to work on it far into the future.

While their projects differ in size, scope and longevity, the Power of Children Award winners profiled in the following pages have one thing in common. Each of them recognized a problem and set out to solve it. Their efforts affected the lives of people in need—sometimes dozens, sometimes hundreds, sometimes thousands. But they all began with the simple desire to help.

~ ~ ~

ASHLEE HAMMER (2005)

"A small act has the potential to grow into a huge movement, if there is heart and dedication behind it."

Project: Aid for Heroes in Afghanistan
- Active from 2004 to 2006
- 140 care packages and letters sent to soldiers in Afghanistan
- 1,100 clothing items donated to Alauddin Orphanage
- 2,600 school supplies given to a new school in Afghanistan
- 200 kits containing 41,000 medical supplies sent to clinics and families in Afghanistan

Imagine being far from home. Wouldn't it be comforting to know that someone was thinking of you? That's the question 7th-grader Ashlee Hammer asked herself when a family friend who was in the U.S. Army was sent to Afghanistan in 2004. He was stationed in that country's capital city, Kabul, 7,000 miles away from his home in Indianapolis. It was early in the war that the United States was fighting against the Taliban, the group then ruling Afghanistan, and Ashlee's friend sent her and her family emails and pictures to let them know he was safe and what he was doing.

That was how Ashlee learned what life was like for soldiers in Afghanistan. Soldiers like Ashlee's friend had to live thousands of miles away from their families. They

Ashlee stands next to a statue of her alma mat[er] mascot in front of the Atherton Union building at Bu[tler] Univers[ity]

also could not make a spur-of-the-moment dash to [a] local store for the things they missed having from home[.]

Ashlee also learned that some Afghan childre[n] lived in orphanages because they had lost their fami-lies and homes to the war. The Alauddin Orphanag[e] did not have enough clothing, soap, or toothpaste fo[r] all 700 children who lived there. It was tough enoug[h] just to provide food and shelter to so many people.

Ashlee wanted to help, so she created a projec[t] called Aid for our Heroes in Afghanistan (AHA)[.] Because soldiers were away from their families[,] Ashlee decided she and her friends would write let-ters to them. Before email, texting, and social media[,] writing letters was how people communicated ove[r]

Ashlee poses with some of the 140 care packages she sent to Afghanistan.

long distances. Although people don't do it as much anymore, writing a letter is still one of the best ways to make the person receiving it feel special.

Since the soldiers were far from home during the holidays, Ashlee also thought they would like care packages. She collected personal care items and food to send to the soldiers. She wrapped them all with red and green ribbons to help cheer them up. Because sending packages so far away was going to be expensive, Ashlee asked local businesses for help. The result was donations of more than $250, which she used to send her packages to Afghanistan.

The care packages were well received and many soldiers wrote back to thank Ashlee for sending them. Still, she realized she could help a lot more people by gathering some of her friends together and asking for donations. She thought about the Afghan children at the Alauddin Orphanage and collected blankets, soap, clothes, and toys for them. Once again she was rewarded for her efforts, this time with the gratitude of the people who ran the orphanage and the children living there.

Ashlee and her classmates got more than they expected from helping others. They learned about Afghan culture through interacting with the children and soldiers who lived there. Also, when Ashlee first started her project, some of her teachers worried that she wanted to do too much. But she showed that through planning and hard work her goals could be accomplished.

A recipient of a prestigious Lilly Endowment Community Scholarship, which paid for four years of undergraduate studies at Butler University in Indianapolis, Ashlee studied elementary education. While preparing to become a teacher, she served as a student ambassador to Japan, a tornado relief volunteer, and a founding member and vice president of fund-raising for the university's Help Heal Haiti chapter. She also collected books, games, and puzzles to donate to local daycare centers, something she says she was inspired to do by her experiences with AHA. A two-time Top 100 student, Ashlee graduated from Butler in 2014 with plans to continue working on behalf of others.

Ashlee said her project taught her that kids can make a difference if they're dedicated to an idea. Despite what others might say, even small acts can have an impact if they're done with care and compassion.

QUESTIONS TO THINK ABOUT
- How did collaborating with other people help Ashlee help others?
- What could you collect that other people need? How would you collect the items?
- Have you ever participated in a donation drive? What did you do?
- What are some local organizations that collect resources in your area? If you don't know, do some research.
- If you could, would you go to another country to help others? Where would you go?

SARAH (BOESING) KELSEY (2006)

"Don't give up on what you're passionate about, even if other people think you look ridiculous."

Project: Break the Grey
- Active from 2006 to 2013
- 300 families served
- Hosted 15 Break the Grey parties
- Raised childhood cancer awareness
- Participated in additional fundraisers for families

Sarah, shown as a 2006 winner, went on to Anderso University in Indiana to become a pediatric nurse. Sh was the graduation speaker for her nursing class

Have you ever had cabin fever? You know that feeling you get after being cooped up inside for days on end while winter winds howl? Imagine feeling like that while lying in a hospital bed.

Sarah Boesing didn't have to imagine it—she experienced it. Born with a chronic kidney disease, Sarah spent a lot of time at Kosair Children's Hospital in Louisville, Kentucky, in the pediatric kidney disease and cancer ward called 7 West. Her doctors told her that her disease was terminal. However, when she was 11 years old, Sarah received a kidney transplant that saved her life.

Her time on 7 West led Sarah to reflect. Because 1 in every 330 Americans develops some form of cancer before the age of 20, there were a lot of other children who wouldn't get the good news that Sarah had gotten when she received her kidney transplant. As she recovered, she began thinking of ways to help them.

That led her to create an event called Break the Grey. She led volunteers from her school's Fellowship of Christian Athletes (FCA) organization to hold the first Break the Grey event in January 2006. Sarah chose January because not many events take place in hospitals then. The holiday parties and gift exchanges are over, and everyone is gearing up for another year. The weather is still cold, cloudy, and grey. Sarah wanted to "break the grey" by giving gifts to the patients receiving treatment as well as to their siblings and parents at a special party thrown just for them.

In order to gather gifts, Sarah set up places for students to donate items at her school. The response was overwhelming. For the first Break the Grey event, Sarah collected so many donations that she gave gifts to all of the 7 West patients and to other patients in the hospital, too.

The patients and their siblings received gift bundles, which included stuffed animals, toys, and candy. The parents were surprised to receive gifts, too—baskets with books, coffee mugs, coffee, tea, mints, and lotion.

Sarah continued planning Break the Grey events until 2013, expanding the program and throwing a party for patients twice a year. She extended the project beyond Kosair Children's Hospital to Riley

Hospital for Children in Indianapolis. In 2013, Break the Grey had its last event, a few months after Sarah had passed her nursing exams and taken a position as a night nurse with Kosair Children's Hospital on 7 West, the same unit where she had spent so much time as a child. At that point she decided that the best way to help patients was to be the best nurse she could be.

Though she experienced some complications after her transplant, Sarah has been disease-and treatment-free since November 2011. Her hospital experiences, as well as her Break the Grey project, inspired her to become a pediatric nurse specializing in hematology and oncology. An accomplished athlete in high school, she attended Anderson University, where she was the graduation speaker for her nursing class.

She credits the Power of Children Award with helping her become a nurse by opening the door to scholarship opportunities. She also said the award allowed her to expand her project to a second hospital.

Along the way she learned she could reach her goals by taking them one step at a time and asking for help when she needed it. For anyone undertaking any task that seems too big to accomplish, Sarah's advice was to do the same. "Work hard, don't give up, and stay humble while you're doing it."

QUESTIONS TO THINK ABOUT

- How do you think Sarah helped others? Was it more than giving gifts?
- What obstacles do you want to overcome? What obstacles do you want to help others overcome?
- How do you like to be cheered up? How do you cheer up others?
- Sarah threw parties to help others. How can you make volunteering fun?
- Have you ever had to visit someone in the hospital? What do you remember? Have you ever had to stay overnight in the hospital? What was that experience like?

MATT CIULLA (2006)

"Join an organization such as the Boy Scouts or Girl Scouts. These organizations are designed to allow you to make connections and learn skills that will enable you to tackle big issues."

Project: Parties Are Lessons in Sharing
- Active from 2006 to 2010
- Helped 35 children
- Created 4 separate events for children

What if you lost everything in a fire or tornado? What if your parents suddenly had no money to put food on the table or to pay for your clothes and school supplies? What if life as you've known it vanished, leaving you with nothing but needs that you couldn't fulfill?

For many children in need, charities, religious organizations, and other nonprofits provide necessities such as food, clothing, and school supplies. The children who need these things really appreciate getting them but they also may feel embarrassed that they need help.

In 2006 Matt Ciulla, an 8th-grader at Sycamore School in Indianapolis, Indiana, discovered a way that he could get resources to children in need without making them feel embarrassed or ashamed about getting help. Better yet, he could do it while providing a lighthearted atmosphere. Matt created a group called Parties Are Lessons in Sharing (PALS), which had three objectives.

The first objective was to throw parties for kids so that they could have some fun. In this way, the children who needed supplies or faced problems in their everyday lives could forget some of their troubles for at least a short time. They could play games and participate in activities. They could concentrate on being kids.

The second objective was to give away a lot of supplies to the people who needed them. The games the children played at the party gave them the chance to win prizes, like coats, clothes, and shoes. Since they

Matt graduated from Vanderbilt University in Nashville, Tennessee, and went on to study law at the University of Notre Dame University in South Bend, Indiana.

won the prizes, they did not feel like they were getting a handout.

The third objective was to get other students who were Matt's age to learn how they could have an impact on their local communities as volunteers. Just like laughter and yawns, volunteering is infectious—seeing someone else do it makes other people do it too. Matt felt a sense of accomplishment as he worked on his project and he wanted to show others that they could feel the same way while making a difference in other people's lives.

To help fund his project, Matt wrote an application for the United Way's Youth as Resources grant. He was awarded the grant and used the funding to throw better and bigger parties. He provided more snacks and prizes for the children who came to the events.

But Matt faced some challenges while trying to make his project a success. He had to develop and manage a budget, which every organization has to do to ensure it has accurate records of how much money it has and how much it spends. He also had to lead and inspire a team to help him with the work. The reward for all his hard work was seeing kids come to an event and leave with things they needed.

Matt used his $2,000 Power of Children grant for another project that was very important to him. When he graduated from Sycamore he attended University High School in Carmel, Indiana, where he was an active member of the Technical Theatre. He wrote a 25-page training manual for the equipment that the drama club used, and then used the grant to renovate part of a building on campus, creating a storage space for the theater. Once again he inspired volunteers to help him with all the labor that was involved.

"The Power of Children Award helped me to understand the grant process, and the impact a grant can have on a project," Matt said later. That knowledge led him to become a member of the Technical Merit Review Committee for the Tennessee Department of Education while he attended Vanderbilt University in Nashville. After graduating from Vanderbilt with a degree in Human and Organizational Development, he decided to become a lawyer. In 2014 he was accepted into Notre Dame University's Law School in South Bend, Indiana.

QUESTIONS TO THINK ABOUT

- How would you give supplies to people who do not want handouts?
- If you wanted to apply for a grant, how would you find one?
- Do you or your family keep a budget? How do you do this?
- Do you volunteer on a regular basis? Do you do it alone or with friends?
- What do you think would be the hardest part of doing a service project? How do you think you could overcome that challenge?
- How could you teach your friends more about volunteering?

RILEY CURRY (2006)

"Never give up; every dream is achievable."

Project: Sunday Breakfast Program

- Established in 2006
- Serves hot breakfast to 50 individuals weekly
- Provides temporary shelter to people who are homeless

The success of Riley's program led to the development of a shelter where people could sleep.

Gathering around a table for a home-cooked meal with family or friends is something millions of people around the world enjoy. But what if you didn't have any food or the money to buy it? What if there is no table to gather around or no home to cook a meal in? What if you had no family or friends to turn to for help?

Unfortunately many Americans face those circumstances every day. One in six have no access to the food they need to lead a healthy life. Most days there are organizations that provide food and shelter to people in need. Yet every Sunday morning, on the way to First Christian Church in Bloomington, Indiana, high school sophomore Riley Curry noticed people asking for money or food.

Riley knew that a growing number of people in his community were hungry. Some were homeless. Some were trying hard just to make ends meet. He wondered why no one was helping them out.

As it turned out, there were a variety of organizations that reached out to people in need. The problem was, many were closed on Sundays. That spurred Riley to action. Working with his parents and his church he started the Sunday Breakfast Program.

The first week that Riley served breakfast at First Christian Church, very few people showed up. But soon the word spread. The next week, Riley and his volunteers served breakfast to 40 people. In addition to the hash browns, eggs, coffee, and juice at breakfast, Riley also packed sack lunches for people to take with them.

As people in his church and community saw what Riley was doing and the impact he was having, they stepped up to help. Riley had so many offers of help that he created a volunteer schedule.

When he was not packing lunches, cooking, or serving breakfast, Riley focused on finding supplies or raising money to buy the food the program needed to feed all of the hungry people who showed up every Sunday. When he didn't get enough donations he and the volunteers had to make meals out of what they had on hand. Sometimes Riley used his own money to purchase the supplies the program needed. Sometimes he struggled to make sure it kept going from week to week.

But it did. In fact, eight years after its 2006 beginning, the Sunday Breakfast Program was continuing to feed the hungry. Along the way Riley lost track of how many people the program had helped.

Thanks in part to winning the Power of Children Award, more people heard about Riley's program. He used the $2,000 grant that came with the award to buy a new freezer, storage cabinets, and kitchen equipment. That meant he could keep more food, store it longer, and prepare it more easily. The Power of

...ley enjoys the company of a good ...iend.

Children Award also led to Riley's project receiving another grant from the City of Bloomington a few months later.

The success of the breakfast program also led to the development of a shelter where people in need could sleep, not just on Sundays but other nights of the week as well. It was a much-needed addition to the community because other shelters in the area were always crowded.

While Riley's program was an ongoing success, his involvement ended when he entered college. The demands of earning an associate's degree from Ivy Tech Community College in Bloomington limited the amount of time he could spend on the program. But his parents remained involved and kept Riley updated on its status. He continues to look for opportunities to help others, keeping in mind his advice to others who are considering projects of their own. "Give even more than you believe you can because it will grow 10 times for every ounce of effort."

QUESTIONS TO THINK ABOUT

- When you go without a meal, how do you feel?
- Does your community have places to help those who need food? What sort of places are they and what help can they provide?
- Are you active in a community, school, or faith group? What could the group do to help get food to the hungry?
- What is the longest you have volunteered in one place? Why is that?

KEEGAN MCCARTHY (2007)

"Nothing is too big. You should never give up."

Project: Keegan's Clan

- Established in 2006
- Raised $370,000 as an organization
- Raised $75,000 as an individual

If you've ever spent any time in a hospital, you know it's no amusement park.

Keegan McCarthy certainly does. In 2006, he was diagnosed with acute lymphocytic leukemia, a cancer that starts with the white blood cells in a person's bone marrow. He was only 11 years old. His test results showed that his cancer was Philadelphia chromosome–positive, meaning that it was spreading faster than usual.

He needed a bone marrow transplant, and his 9-year-old sister Shannon was a match for the procedure. After his bone marrow transplant, Keegan was at Riley Hospital for Children In Indianapolis for 45 days. A lot of that time he felt sick from additional radiation treatments to kill the cancer cells.

When he was able to go home, Keegan spent the summer of 2006 indoors. Only healthy friends were permitted to visit him because his immune system was weak after the transplant and radiation treatments. He missed an entire year of school, too, but he was able to keep up academically with the help of tutors who came to his home.

Throughout his ordeal, however, Keegan kept a positive attitude. From the beginning, he was confident that he would win his fight with cancer. He said, "I'm not going to die. The cancer is going to die!"

As he recovered, Keegan wanted to find a way to raise money for cancer research. He did not want anyone else to go through what he had experienced.

Keegan and his family created Keegan's Clan to do just that. Working through the St. Baldrick's Foundation, a national organization dedicated to raising money to help children with cancer, Keegan asked his friends, family, and others to join with him to raise funds for cancer research. To raise money, he asked people to shave their heads.

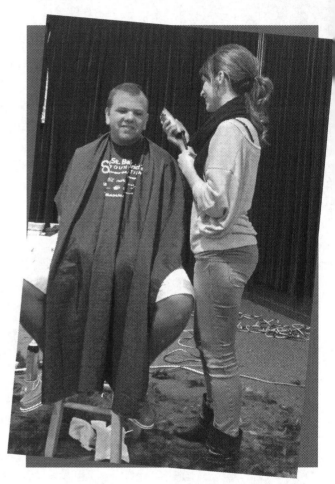

Keegan has his head shaved every year to raise more funds for his project.

People who volunteered to shave their heads not only honored Keegan's Irish heritage at events held around St. Patrick's Day, but also showed support for children with cancer, who sometimes lose their hair due to the radiation or chemotherapy treatments. But most important, volunteers raised thousands of dollars for cancer research.

As a survivor, Keegan made it his mission to raise awareness of childhood cancer. He marched in parades, raised money through raffles and silent auctions, shaved thousands of heads, and befriended children going through treatment as he did. As he has grown older, though, he discovered another passion: working with young people.

He experimented with new projects and activities that would allow him to have an impact on others' lives. As the manager for the basketball and softball teams at Roncalli High School in Indianapolis, Keegan took what he'd learned and began coaching basketball and softball for younger kids. Because of his experience in overcoming adversity, he realized he could be a role model. While teaching the fundamentals of a sport he also began teaching the fundamentals of life—especially the importance of maintaining a positive outlook.

Even when Keegan enrolled in the University of Indianapolis, majoring in accounting, he made time to continue his coaching duties. Rather than being discouraged by his battle with cancer, he used it to his

Keegan shows that you are never too young to make a difference.

advantage, becoming an example of the power of perseverance and positivity.

QUESTIONS TO THINK ABOUT

- Do you talk to your parents about your family's medical history or genetic health issues?
- Have you ever donated to a cause or organization? What was it? Why did you decide to donate?
- Would you ever shave your head in support of a cause or to support a friend who had cancer?
- What does heritage mean? What do you know about your heritage?
- Do you play sports or do activities with a coach? What do you like about your coach? What does he or she teach you besides your activity?

EVANNE OFFENBACKER (2007)

"ENJOY! As in, enjoy the moment that you are in, enjoy the opportunities and the people around you, and don't forget to stop and take time to smile, laugh, and enjoy the moments you are in!"

Project: Straight 2 the Streets

- Active from 2007 to 2009
- Made weekly visits to downtown urban areas
- Built relationships with people who were homeless
- Provided meals and clothing to those in need

Evanne sits among many of her young charges Mauritius Island in Thailar

People who live in cities have advantages that smaller communities may lack. They have access to jobs, health care, libraries, museums, stores, and public transportation. They have options for education, recreation, and social services. For many people cities are alive with opportunities.

But Evanne Offenbacker noticed that sometimes living in a place with a lot of resources wasn't enough. A resident of Indianapolis, the 12th largest city in the United States, she realized that some of her city's opportunities were lost on people who couldn't take advantage of them.

One day, while downtown with her church group, Evanne noticed a homeless man sitting on the steps of the Soldiers & Sailors Monument. Suddenly she found herself asking questions she never had asked before. Why was the man homeless? What would he need to no longer be homeless? What were some challenges he faced every day? How could other people help? Why didn't they help? Why didn't *she*?

Walking up to the man, Evanne struck up a conversation. That experience showed her that building relationships was a great way to directly influence the lives of people in need, which became the basis for

Evanne strikes a pose and contemplates the meaning of life.

Straight 2 the Streets, an organization Evanne founded to assist the homeless.

During the two years that Straight 2 the Streets was active, Evanne used donations she received to

anne jumps for joy with students in Thailand.

provide food, clothes, shoes, and water to people who needed them the most. She and a group of friends went downtown weekly to distribute the donations.

In keeping with her belief that building relationships was necessary and beneficial to everyone involved, Evanne and her friends used any money that Straight 2 the Streets received to buy home-cooked meals for the people they met on the streets or to purchase something that a person needed. She even provided a bus ticket to Florida so one of the people she met on the street could visit family members.

From her work Evanne discovered that giving without any expectation of getting something in return was a great way to improve people's lives, hers included. It also meant being on the lookout for any new adventures and opportunities that would encourage her to continue doing that. She loved spreading joy, love, and laughter.

After she finished her project, Evanne took her passion for helping others with her around the world. She spent several weeks in Thailand at a small orphanage, where she had the opportunity to teach young children soccer, English, and painting. She also took her iPod and taught students how to dance like Americans.

An art education major at Indiana University's Herron School of Art and Design in Indianapolis, Evanne's plan for the future was to continue her travels, reaching out to people in need wherever she found herself.

QUESTIONS TO THINK ABOUT

- Have you ever noticed someone who seemed to need help? What were your first impressions?
- What type of supplies do you think would be the most important for people who are homeless?
- How do you think someone becomes homeless? If you aren't sure, search online or call a homeless shelter to find out.
- Spend a little time reading some news stories. Search for world or community issues that affect a lot of people. Pick an issue. What are three things you could do to help? Share what you find and discuss it with a friend, family member, or teacher.

BRANDON TAYLOR (2007)

"What truly measures the impact on someone's life is the thought and feeling that was put forth."

Project: Kids 4 Kidz Foundation

- Active from 2005 to 2011
- Helped 100 youths and families
- Raised $10,000 in grants and donations
- Delivered gifts during the holidays
- Reached out to children and senior citizens

The famous architect Frank Lloyd Wright inspired Brandon Taylor to provide children in hospitals with a positive and memorable experience. "The thing always happens that you really believe in," Wright once said, "and the belief in a thing makes it happen." Thanks to Wright, Brandon believed he could make a positive change in others' lives and that belief led him to make an impact on others.

It started when Brandon was in Methodist Hospital's pediatric unit in Merrillville, Indiana, in the summer of 2004. He noticed there weren't many toys for the young patients to play with. After he recovered from his own illness, Brandon created the Kids 4 Kidz Foundation to give the young patients in the hospital something fun to do during their stay.

He started by delivering Christmas presents and Easter baskets to children hospitalized at Methodist. But Brandon's project soon grew to be much more. As it gained attention and support, he began reaching out to more people. He delivered turkey dinners to senior citizen residents at the AHEPA Apartments in Merrillville on Thanksgiving.

Kids 4 Kidz also began providing activities for teens over the summer. Brandon developed drug and alcohol awareness campaigns, encouraging others to live a healthy lifestyle. His community service efforts, as well as his academic achievements, resulted in his selection as one of 2009's Coca-Cola Scholars.

After graduating from high school, he passed the foundation to his sister, Marissa. She continued it for two

Seen here in 2007, Brandon went on to graduate from Cornell University in Ithaca, New York, and set his sights on running a nonprofit organization

years, but after she graduated, Kids 4 Kidz suspended operations. But Brandon didn't. While attending Cornell University in Ithaca, New York, he traveled to Rome, Italy, to deliver food, clothing, and blankets to people who were homeless and to Sakon Nakhon, Thailand, to work on a local business development project. Those experiences motivated him to take a new direction in his efforts to help others.

After finishing his degree in Urban and Regional Studies from Cornell in 2013, Brandon set his sights on running a nonprofit organization focused on buying vacant properties in poor communities and transforming them into communal spaces and housing for at-risk families. To prepare himself, he took a job as a community development associate with a nonprofit organization in New York City, the first step in a process of gaining the knowledge and experience he knew he would need to achieve his goal.

Whenever he was discouraged in his efforts, Brandon turned to a quote from another famous individual—anthropologist Margaret Mead. She said: "Never doubt that a small group of thoughtful, committed citizens can change the world. Indeed it is the only thing that ever has."

QUESTIONS TO THINK ABOUT

- Have you ever spent time in a hospital? If so, how did it make you feel?
- Did you have a favorite toy growing up? What do you remember about the toy? How would you have felt if you lost it?
- What, or who, do you think makes up your community? Why?
- Have you ever had anything bad happen to you? How did you face it? Did anyone do anything to make you feel better?
- What does the word *communal* mean? How does *communal* relate to community?

KYLE GOUGH (2008)

"Scale an issue down to a manageable size, and do not be afraid to ask others to help you along the way."

Project: PCs for Youth
- Established in 2006
- Provided 500 computers to children in need
- Held an annual fund-raising dinner
- Relied on 12 dedicated volunteers
- Served 6 counties

It's hard to imagine life without a computer—or two or three—near at hand. But in the United States and all around the world there are millions of children to whom owning a computer is as alien as piloting a spaceship.

Having their own computers allows young people to use programs that stimulate learning. They can conduct research, write reports, collaborate on projects, and analyze data. A computer is a tool that allows a child to explore the world outside his or her own door. Without a computer a child has limited access to the advantages of living in a digital era. The gap between those who have computers and connection to the Internet and those who don't is known as the digital divide.

As a sophomore at Westview High School in Topeka, Indiana, Kyle Gough was bothered by the idea of a digital divide. His desire to eliminate it became the basis for PCs for Youth, the organization he founded to provide computers to kids without them.

He started with 15 donated computers he received from an organization in Fort Wayne, Indiana. In his parents' basement, Kyle refurbished them, doing everything from erasing their hard drives to reinstalling their operating systems. He then installed programs such as Microsoft Word or open-source software, and they were ready to be given away.

Kyle set up an application process for students who wanted a computer. He tried to give computers

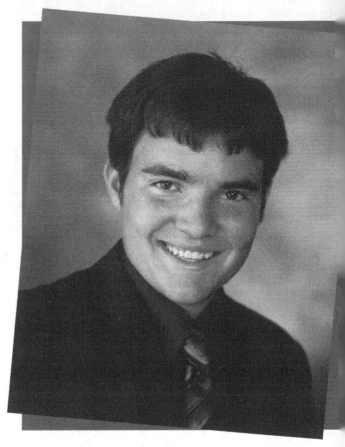

Kyle was valedictorian of his high school class, graduated from DePauw University, and went on to study law at Michigan State University.

to those who needed them the most, like high school seniors graduating and going to college. Winning the Power of Children Award gained more attention for PCs for Youth, which led to more donated computers. The Power of Children grant helped Kyle pay for software that many of the computers needed.

Knowing that a good way to encourage people to keep their word is to ask them to sign a contract, Kyle required recipients of his computers to sign a document stating they would use them for educational purposes only. Not for gaming or streaming videos, not for online shopping or personal blogging, not for entertainment purposes of any kind—strictly for education. The students who received computers were so delighted to have them that they gladly signed Kyle's pledge.

One of the first computers Kyle gave away went to a 12-year-old girl living in a rundown duplex with several siblings. He delivered the computer and made sure it was set up properly. Knowing the computer would give them a chance to do school work better and faster, the girl and her siblings planned to use it when they were home alone while their parents worked.

A few weeks later Kyle followed up with the girl, contacting her to make sure that everything was going well. She said the computer was running perfectly and that her grades had improved. Hundreds of computer donations later, Kyle had plenty more stories of the positive impact PCs for Youth had on young lives.

Winning the Power of Children Award put Kyle in touch with lawyers who helped PCs for Youth obtain its nonprofit status. Valedictorian of Westview's class of 2009, Kyle headed off to Greencastle, Indiana, where he attended DePauw University, majoring in political science and history. Following his graduation from DePauw, he went on to law school at Michigan State University's College of Law in East Lansing, Michigan, after which he said he hoped to get a master's degree in computer science.

While Kyle still volunteered with the organization when he could, he left it up to others to continue what he started. As of 2014 PCs for Youth was going strong, inspired by Kyle's vision of eliminating the digital divide by providing computers to children all over the world.

QUESTIONS TO THINK ABOUT

- Do you use a computer at school and/or at home? Could you complete your assignments if you didn't have access to a computer?
- What are contracts? What is the purpose of a contract? If you aren't sure, search online or ask a teacher or family member for more information.
- Application processes are not all alike. Have you ever applied for anything? What information did you need to give? Why do you think you were asked for it?

KAYLEE SHIRRELL (2009)

"If you are passionate about something, nothing in the world can stop you."

Project: Hats of Hope
- Established in 2008
- Donated 15,000 hats
- Trained 500 people to make hats
- Provided materials to those who want to make hats on their own
- Created multiple drop-off locations for people to donate hats

Kaylee gives a speech at the White House. H volunteerism spurred the donation of 15,000 hats people undergoing cancer treatmer

Cancer patients are often treated with chemotherapy and/or radiation to destroy the cancerous cells that are making them sick. Unfortunately, one of the side effects of those treatments is hair loss. When Kaylee Shirrell's grandmother lost her hair, Kaylee knitted her a hat, which her grandmother really liked. That one hat soon turned into 50 more for other cancer patients. And those 50 hats soon turned into thousands.

The result was Hats of Hope, a project that Kaylee created after deciding that if her grandmother appreciated having a handmade hat, other cancer patients probably would, too. The Brownsburg, Indiana High School junior thought she would team up with the store that had sold her grandmother a wig, offering to give hats to 50 people who bought a wig. That would give them the option to wear the wig, a hat, or both. Having something handmade would also remind them that others supported them and wanted them to get better.

But the store had closed. It seemed Kaylee's plan was stalled until she met a nurse who worked at the Hendricks Regional Health Cancer Center in Danville, Indiana. Hendricks had a program called "Look Good, Feel Better." Kaylee thought her hats were perfect for the program. She delivered her first batch of handmade hats on December 8, 2008, and the hats made such an impact on the lives of patients that Kaylee knew she had to find a way to make more.

As a Girl Scout, she turned to other Scouts as well as to friends and family, offering to teach anyone who was interested how to knit hats. While Kaylee used a

Kaylee stands next to her inspiration for Hats of Hope, her grandmother, Barbara Soeurt.

loom, which allowed her to make hats very quickly, she knew knitting by hand would be an inexpensive way to get others to make them. She held her first workshop at the local public library. Before long, she had taught hundreds of people how to knit hats, all of which they donated to patients.

Her efforts didn't go unnoticed. As a senior in high school she was selected for *Parade Magazine*'s first High School Service Team. That led her to a meeting with Vice President Joe Biden and an opportunity to deliver a speech at the White House. She also received the American Red Cross Hall of Fame Award in 2011.

Following her 2010 high school graduation Kaylee enrolled at Indiana University-Purdue University Indianapolis (IUPUI), using her Power of Children scholarship to help her get a degree in psychology. While at IUPUI (she graduated in May 2014), she continued making hats, though at a slower pace than before. She also took part in campus service events, including an annual dance marathon that raised money for the Riley Hospital for Children in Indianapolis.

While she was happy to help everyone who benefited from Hats for Hope, Kaylee envisioned a day when the organization will no longer be needed because medical researchers have cured cancer.

QUESTIONS TO THINK ABOUT

- Have you ever made anything from scratch? What did you make? Was it better than something similar from a store? Why or why not?
- Who was the last person you helped? What did you do for them and how did you feel afterward?
- Could the things you make end up helping others? How?
- What hobbies do you enjoy that could be used to help others? What sort of fun activities could also be volunteer work?
- How would you help someone who is not having fun with a service project?

KAYLIN FANTA (2010)

"You should dream big and tell everyone your dreams. You would be surprised who will help you if they know that you are putting forth the effort."

Project: Watts Backpack Baggers
- Established in 2003
- Donated 1,500 backpacks with school supplies
- Raises money through social events
- Makes donations year-round
- Awarded two additional grants to expand

Kaylin Fanta never expected to win an award for something she had been doing since she was 8 years old. In fact, when Kaylin got started giving children the supplies they needed to be successful in school, she was just a kid who was bored during summer vacation.

That summer, Kaylin held a talent show in her neighborhood. Not only did she and her neighbors have fun, she also raised $50 through the show. She then used the money to purchase school supplies for 10 children who needed them.

Why did she spend the money on school supplies? Kaylin remembered going to a food bank with her mother. She asked her mom how the children there could afford school supplies if their families could not afford food. When her mother told her that the children might not have school supplies for the next school year, Kaylin knew she wanted to help.

The first 10 students Kaylin helped were so appreciative that she decided to do it again the following school year. She named her project Watts Backpack Baggers after her subdivision, Watts, in St. John, Indiana. She collected backpacks and told everyone she knew what she was doing. People dropped off backpacks at her house, and Kaylin sewed up any holes, making the packs look almost new.

In order to raise money for backpacks and school supplies, Kaylin held craft shows and ran lemonade stands. She used the money to buy supplies to fill the backpacks people had donated. At the end of her second summer, she gave backpacks and school supplies to 25 kids.

Kaylin and her sister teach a young volunteer how to he

Word spread, and the next year Kaylin got 50 backpacks from students in her school. She held an ice cream social to raise money for supplies, and someone gave her $85 for a chocolate sundae! That year, Kaylin provided backpacks and supplies for half the children who used the local food pantry.

Wanting to do even better the next year, she asked two schools' students for their backpacks. She collected supplies all summer. At the end of her third summer, she prepared 100 backpacks for children in need—helping every child at the food pantry that first had inspired her to action.

She made such an impact on her community that when the Indiana town of Munster flooded, Kaylin was asked if she had any supplies for kids who lost everything in the flood. She gave them all of the supplies she had collected for that year. When executives at Target, the nationwide store chain, found out that she gave her supplies away, they decided to match her donation. That way, the children Kaylin helped at the food pantry did not have to go without supplies that year, and the children who needed help in Munster got supplies too.

Kaylin's work helped children in need and also united a community around a cause. As of 2014 she was continuing her project, which had become a year-round effort, donating clothing and coats as well as school supplies. Her Power of Children grant allowed her to get more people involved, expand her project, and worry less about raising money. She also turned her project into a nonprofit organization, allowing donations to be tax deductible.

Taking advantage of the Power of Children scholarship, Kaylin began attending Indiana University-Purdue University Indianapolis (IUPUI) in the fall of 2014. A Girl Scout and a member of the National Honor Society, she planned to major in nursing and minor in business. She also planned to continue her support for food drives, peer tutoring, and packing backpacks throughout college.

ylin attended IUPUI thanks to her
CA scholarship.

QUESTIONS TO THINK ABOUT

- What is something that a lot of people throw away that could be reused or donated?
- Kaylin repaired the backpacks before giving them away. Do you know how to repair anything that someone else might need?
- What are some things that people use only during certain times of the year? How could they be repurposed?

BENJAMIN GORMLEY (2010)

"If you show up, have an open mind, and care about issues and other people, you will see a way to contribute."

Project: Operation Backpack for Indy's Homeless
- Established in 2008
- Distributed 800 backpacks

There's never a good time to lose someone you love, but for Benjamin Gormley it happened when he was only 10 years old. His father died. Yet he found a way to turn his loss into an opportunity to honor the man who had taught him that helping others is a path to joy. Having helped his dad serve meals to the homeless at his church, he wanted to continue doing projects that benefited others in need.

When Benjamin was 12 years old and searching for something meaningful to do for his Eagle Scout project, he remembered helping his father at their church. That's when he hit upon the notion of collecting backpacks and filling them with items that would be useful to the homeless population in Indianapolis. Not only that, but they would be easy to carry around.

To make certain the backpacks contained the most useful sorts of things, Benjamin called shelters in downtown Indianapolis. He met with the director and outreach workers at the Indianapolis Homeless Initiative Program. Not only did they help Benjamin understand the problem of homelessness better, the Indianapolis Homeless Initiative Program agreed to help distribute his backpacks.

Benjamin's project, Operation Backpack for Indy's Homeless, had an initial goal of packing and distributing 50 backpacks. The backpacks contained things like gloves, socks, toothbrushes, and toothpaste, deodorant, and towels. What's more, a pack could serve as a pillow at night, a briefcase for important papers, a hygiene kit, a lunchbox, or a safe place to store personal belongings.

Some of the backpacks that people donated to Benjamin were more appropriate for children than adults. In those backpacks he included a stuffed animal to help lift the spirits of children who were homeless.

Within a few months, Benjamin met his goal. He got his Eagle Scout rank and could have ended Operation Backpack. However, he felt that it would be unfair to the people who needed help if he quit just because he got what he wanted out of the project.

So he kept going. As of 2014 Benjamin had distributed hundreds of backpacks, many of them

Benjamin was named American Legion Eagle Scout of the Year. He donated more than 800 backpacks to Indianapolis' homeless.

stocked with items he was able to buy with his Power of Children grant. Winner of multiple awards and certified in a variety of life-saving skills, he believed that his impact went further than helping the homeless. He said he hoped that the other young volunteers who helped him with his project were also inspired to do more for their communities.

After graduating from Carmel High School in Carmel, Indiana, in 2014, Benjamin headed to Purdue University in West Lafayette. He intended to major in economics and minor in German while completing the university's Entrepreneurship and Innovation certificate. One of the guiding principles he adopted was to leave things better than he found them. From a campsite to a community, he said, everyone has the power to improve things for the people who come after them. His father would be proud.

Benjamin went on to become a student at Purdue University in West Lafayette, Indiana.

QUESTIONS TO THINK ABOUT

- What types of things do you carry in your backpack? Why do you need them with you?
- Do you like to do activities with your parents or other adult family members? What do you do? Why do you like doing these activities together?
- Have you ever started a project that was supposed to be short-term but decided to keep working on it? Why did you keep it going?
- If Ben had not had help getting the backpacks to those in need, how else could he have accomplished his goal?
- What are some types of service organizations that young people can join?

CLAIRE HELMEN (2010)

"The most important thing is to take one step at a time. You can't move a mountain in a day."

Project: Claire's Comfort for Kids
- Active from 2007 to 2013
- Made and distributed 3,600 blankets

Being wrapped in a blanket makes anyone feel warm and cozy. But in a traumatic situation a blanket is even more comforting.

Twelve-year-old Claire Helmen's mother worked with victims of domestic violence. As a result, Claire knew there were children in tough situations who were scared.

She knew that police and firefighters were often the first people on the scene of traumatic situations that involved scared children. That gave her an idea. She decided she would collect blankets and give them to officers and firefighters to give them to children in those situations.

To move from idea to reality Claire had to get a steady supply of blankets to give to first responders. She pitched her idea to the Junior Achievement Summer Biz Camp, an educational camp in Indianapolis, Indiana that helped students create their own businesses and invent new products. They liked her idea and used it for their social entrepreneurship project. Claire taught the campers how to make blankets, and Junior Achievement funded the project. This effort resulted in 500 blankets!

Claire completed her project by producing another 600 blankets.

Claire's proudest moment came when the National Football League's Indianapolis Colts chose her organization, Claire's Comfort for Kids, as their game day charity. She raised enough money that she was able to make hundreds of blankets. She also led a summer workshop at The Children's Museum of Indianapolis, home of the Power of Children Awards, which resulted in 600 more blankets.

Claire's organization was also listed on the Indiana Coalition Against Domestic Violence's website. This gave others the chance to begin their own chapters to create more blankets.

In addition to soothing frightened children, Claire's Comfort for Kids helped its founder overcome her hesitancy about public speaking and media interviews, both of which she had to do to promote her project. She said she realized she had a responsibility to be a role model for others wanting to get involved in community service.

A 2014 graduate of Bishop Chatard High School in Indianapolis, Claire headed to Indiana University in Bloomington. Winner of a National Spirit of Anne Frank Scholarship for her community service, Claire made it possible for thousands of first responders to provide comfort to children when they needed it most.

Claire continued to radiate sunshine during her senior year in high school.

QUESTIONS TO THINK ABOUT

- What types of things could you do to help people rescued by first responders?
- Claire's project included handwritten notes with the blankets. What do you think is written on the notes?
- What do you find comforting? Why do you think that is?
- How do you comfort others when they are sad, in pain, scared, or sick?

ASHLEY SLAYTON (2010)

"All it takes is some hard work and planning to make an impact or difference in the community."

Project: Nana's Cancer Miracles

- Established in 2008
- Helped 5,000 patients with cancer
- Helped 300 children during Christmas time

One of the most life-changing medical diagnoses anyone can receive is cancer. A lot of questions immediately come up. What type of cancer? How advanced is it? What treatment is available? What side effects are there? And perhaps the most important question of all: How successful is the treatment?

A person with cancer will be concerned for his or her own mental and physical well-being, but will also wonder how the coming battle will be viewed by family members. Will they be supportive? Will they see the person rather than the disease? Will they want to help or avoid the cancer patient?

When Ashley Slayton found out her grandmother, whom she called Nana, was sick, she held her hand and said, "We can get through this together."

Ashley's love and support for her grandmother inspired her to create Nana's Cancer Miracles. The project began simply enough. The medication that Ashley's Nana took caused her to lose her hair. Many cancer patients experience hair loss during treatment. Some choose to wear wigs. Since Nana's insurance did not cover the cost of wigs Ashley saved some money and bought two wigs to cheer her up.

The smile on her Nana's face made Ashley realize that she could have the same impact on others going through similar challenges. As a 6th-grader at Decatur Middle School in Indianapolis, Indiana, Ashley wanted to do more, but she had no idea how to get started. So she did some research to learn how to run a charity. Then she wrote down goals she wanted to accomplish and a mission statement to guide her.

But one of the biggest challenges Ashley had to overcome was her shyness. She was nervous about asking others for help and about talking in front of a lot of people. However, her desire to help others motivated her and with practice, she overcame her fears. So much so that she became a recognized cancer advocate. She was even invited to be the keynote speaker for the kickoff of the 2010 Relay for Life, an annual event in which teams of people run and walk around a track for 24 hours.

Ashley prepares to share some of her many Easter baskets with cancer patients.

From a small organization helping a few people, Nana's Cancer Miracles turned into something much larger. As of 2014 it was assisting patients (including children) at seven cancer centers in Indiana, with thousands of donated wigs, hats, stuffed animals, and cards. Her organization teamed up with Decatur Middle School to create an official donation site at the school. Ashley donated her Power of Children Award grant to the Central Indiana Cancer Research Foundation to help find a cure for her grandmother's cancer. She also planned to use the scholarship that comes with the award to attend Indiana University-Purdue University Indianapolis (IUPUI) once she graduated from high school in 2015.

Unfortunately, Ashley's grandmother lost her battle with cancer. Ashley put her project on hold while her Nana was very sick and became a care-giver for both of her grandparents. Although such a loss created a new challenge to overcome as Ashley grieved, serving others remained important to her.

Ashley and her family celebrate another holiday to share joy with others.

She concentrated on her Relay for Life team and continued to seek ways to help others.

QUESTIONS TO THINK ABOUT

- Do you know anyone who is battling a serious illness? If so, what can do you do to help that person? What can you learn from him or her?
- What is a mission statement? Write a mission statement to solve a problem you think is important to solve.
- How do you feel about public speaking? What do you think are the most important skills a public speaker has to have? What is a keynote speaker?
- Do you know what running a charity requires? Where can you go to find more information?
- What are some ways that shy people can help as volunteers?

LIZ NIEMIEC (2011)

"We need to constantly remember that there is more to life than our problems, our issues, ourselves."

Project: Little Wish Foundation

- Established in 2010
- Granted 250 wishes for kids at 3 Indiana hospitals
- Raised $250,000 through special events and sales of bracelets and T-shirts

Max Olson was just an ordinary 7-year-old boy with an ordinary hope. He really wanted a puppy. It wasn't much to ask, especially for someone with a rare form of kidney cancer called Wilms' tumor, which affects about 500 Americans every year, 75 percent of them children. Max got his puppy, though he didn't live long enough to enjoy growing up with a dog for a pal.

Liz splits her time between her studies in Arts Administration at Butler University and her Little Wishes Foundation.

Max's mother was a 5th-grade school teacher, and one of her former students, Liz Niemiec, was particularly close with Max and his family. When Max passed away in 2010, Liz remembered how happy he was when his parents got him his puppy. Even though he was sick, for just a little while he was able to forget about his illness and play with his dog.

After Max's funeral, Liz—who was then a junior at Michigan City High School in Michigan City, Indiana—told her mother she was going to create a foundation. She wanted to do something for children who were sick and in need of something comforting, like the puppy had been for Max.

After a couple of months of research, paperwork and effort, Liz's nonprofit organization, the Little Wish Foundation, was born. Since Max had been so happy to get a dog, Liz wanted to grant "little wishes" like Max's for other children.

By the time Liz won her Power of Children Award, the Little Wish Foundation had granted wishes for 12 children. They received iPods, laptops, Blu-ray players, gaming systems, and other toys. In the years that followed, Liz's organization helped more than 200 children and their families. Liz recruited volunteers from local schools and organizations, and she planned fund-raising events like hog roasts, wine tastings, and 5K runs throughout the year.

The recipient of several awards and scholarships for her work with the Little Wish Foundation, Liz graduated with academic honors from high school in 2012 and enrolled at Butler University in Indianapolis. Majoring in arts administration, Liz split her time between her foundation and her studies. She intended to apply what she learned in college to expand the foundation on a global scale. To do that she first planned to expand the organization outside of Indiana, building relationships that will result in a national program with an international reach.

As of 2014 the Little Wish Foundation had already started expanding. From its initial focus on granting wishes for patients at the South Bend Children's Hospital, it was doing the same for patients at both Riley Hospital for Children and Peyton Manning Children's Hospital in Indianapolis. As it continued to grow, Liz vowed never to forget how it started—with a boy and his dog.

QUESTIONS TO THINK ABOUT

- Do you think it is important to grant wishes to children who are sick? What about children in general? Why or why not?
- If you could make a wish, what would it be and why? How can you make your wish happen?
- Have you ever had a wish come true? What was that experience like? Was your wish everything you hoped for?
- What are some wishes that other people have? Ask your family and friends what theirs are. How could you make someone else's wish come true?

JILL OSTERHUS (2011)

*"The best thing you can do is persevere.
Making a difference isn't easy, but in the end, it will be more than worth it."*

Project: Educate Jamaica
- Established in 2009
- Developed a relationship with Church Hill Primary, a Jamaican school
- Wrote letters to sponsors to pay for shipping costs
- Teamed up with U-Haul to ship books to Miami for shipment to Jamaica
- Donated 1,400 pounds of books

When people go on a vacation, some of them explore where they are, learning about the history, culture, and customs of a place. Others just want to have fun. Still others seek out opportunities to get to know the people who live in tourist destinations.

For Jill Osterhus, her vacation to Jamaica in 2008 made her ask what she could do to help people less fortunate than herself. Going from the airport to the resort where her family was staying, Jill saw firsthand the effects of poverty on Jamaicans, 16.5 percent of whom are impoverished.

It was not until Jill met two Jamaican women, Janet and Angela, that she realized what she could do to help. One day while they braided her hair, Jill struck up a conversation, asking what she could bring the next time her family visited Jamaica. Both Janet and Angela said that what they needed more than anything else was textbooks and school supplies for their children.

Jill's family thought it was a good idea to help and suggested that Jill bring some of their old books on their next trip to Jamaica. Jill, however, wanted to make an impact on the lives of Jamaicans sooner than that.

Returning home to Munster, Indiana, she realized that when the school year ended at the local high school, a lot of kids threw away gently used school supplies and textbooks. That spring when students cleaned out their lockers, Jill was there to gather any unused school supplies. She also contacted her younger sister's school and found out which children's

Jill, in 2011, as she educated Jamaicans.

books, dictionaries, magazines, and other materials teachers and students were going to get rid of at the end of the year.

That was the birth of Educate Jamaica, a project that Jill, who was in 7th grade at the time, developed to help Jamaican students. In her first attempt she collected more than 500 pounds of books and school supplies.

That presented her with a new problem. It was really expensive to send 500 pounds of books and supplies to another country. Luckily Jill's grandfather discovered the Sandals Foundation, an organization that reaches out to countries in the Caribbean. Jill emailed the organization and asked if there was any way it could help. Sure, was the reply. All she had to do was get her packages to the foundation's office in Miami, Florida, and they would be shipped to Jamaica.

So Jill and her dad set off on a road trip from Munster to Miami with a car full of packages. But her efforts didn't end there. After receiving her Power of Children Award, Jill used her grant to purchase laptops, books, and school supplies for the children at Church Hill Primary in Jamaica.

Excited to know that she helped the lives of others, Jill was surprised by how many wonderful people she met along the way. There were the people who donated supplies, the people who helped her ship materials to Jamaica, and the people who ran their own service organizations. All of them reinforced the importance of turning compassion into action.

Following her graduation from high school in 2014, Jill headed off to Purdue University in West Lafayette, Indiana, with plans to continue her philanthropic work. She hoped one day to help rebuild deteriorating schoolhouses around the world, as well as to continue providing books and supplies to students in need.

shares a story with her Jamaican friends.

QUESTIONS TO THINK ABOUT

- Have you ever done something that inspired friends or family members to help others? Has someone else inspired you to help others? Who was it and how did they inspire you?
- Do you know of any neighborhood near you that could use help? What can you do for them?
- Have you ever met someone from a different country or culture? You could have met them on a trip, in your classroom, or in your neighborhood. What did you learn from them?
- What are some things you have that others do not? What do you think are the basic things everyone should have?

KRYSTAL SHIRRELL (2011)

"Think big! There is no limit for how much you can accomplish."

Project: VETSupport
- Established in 2009
- Sent 1,000 care packages overseas
- Held social events to distribute items to soldiers

Volunteering is something that runs in the Shirrell family. Krystal's sister, Kaylee, was a 2009 Power of Children Winner for her project called Hats of Hope.

Although Krystal helped out on her sister's project, she wanted to do something of her own. At one of her sister's hat-making workshops she found out about a problem that she felt she could help solve.

Some people who are sick need to have a procedure called dialysis. Dialysis removes waste and extra water from blood when a person's kidneys are not working correctly. One of the side-effects of dialysis is that it often makes patients cold.

Krystal knew that, as a result of injuries sustained in battle or medical problems that developed later, a lot of military veterans undergo dialysis. To thank them for their service she made patriotic blankets for them. She initially called her project LAP PALS and made it her Girl Scout Gold Award project.

However, when she delivered the blankets she learned about Domiciliary Care for Homeless Veterans, a service center in Indianapolis, Indiana. Krystal did some research and learned that on any given night over 700,000 people in the United States are homeless. Veterans make up 25 percent of that number.

That is when LAP PALS transformed into VETSupport, which stood for "Veterans have Earned our Thanks and Support." Suddenly, the project was about a lot more than making blankets. It was about giving homeless veterans support as they got back on their feet.

Krystal, who was a sophomore at Brownsburg High School in Brownsburg, Indiana, at the time, enlisted the help of other student volunteers to continue delivering blankets and personally thanking each veteran they visited, and to collect needed items for the Domiciliary. She hosted monthly Bingo nights for residents and gave away the items as prizes. She also worked with volunteers on writing grants to help fund VETSupport's efforts.

Krystal is at the University of Iowa on a combination athletic-academic scholarship.

To extend her reach Krystal got elementary school students involved. She sent out thousands of coloring sheets. This provided teachers with an opportunity to teach their students about homelessness. It also gave the students a chance to thank veterans for their service. Also, much like her sister's project, Krystal's program benefited the people who volunteered. For example, she taught a knitting group at a senior center how to make blankets. The time-consuming process was therapeutic for the seniors and helped younger knitters develop patience.

For her work on behalf of veterans, Krystal was selected as Indiana's Top High School Youth Volunteer in 2012, which led to her receiving the Prudential Spirit of Community Award. In turn that resulted in an invitation to meet with President

Barack Obama at the White House. Knowing she was going to Washington, D.C., Krystal made arrangements to visit Walter Reed Memorial Hospital, where many of the most seriously injured service men and women receive medical care. That visit motivated her to start collecting donations for those patients, too.

Following her high school graduation (with academic honors) in 2012, Krystal headed to the University of Iowa on a combination athletic-academic scholarship. But her departure didn't mark the end of VETSupport. As of 2014 it was still active, the result of an arrangement Krystal made with the Brownsburg Community School Corporation to continue her project.

Krystal meets President Barack Obama.

stal speaks with New York Giants arterback Eli Manning. She has been ognized by various organizations for commitment to soldiers overseas.

She also made sure that an annual Support Our Troops and Veterans collection drive still took place and monthly Bingo for Homeless Veterans events also continued to distribute items to veterans. Krystal collected supplies for the Wounded Warriors project and created care packages for troops stationed overseas with the Military Support Group of Brownsburg.

Studying to be a doctor of pharmacy, Krystal hoped to work with the Department of Veterans Affairs, allowing her to go on helping veterans directly. She also planned to keep up her volunteer work with the Domiciliary, and to continue looking for ways to help veterans.

"I have met soldiers and veterans whom I still stay in touch with and consider great friends," she said of her experiences. "Through my project I have been able to change lives, but more important, I have had my life changed."

QUESTIONS TO THINK ABOUT

- Do you know anyone who is a military veteran? Talk with him or her about what it was like adjusting to civilian life after leaving the service.
- What challenges do veterans face once they leave the military? Why do you think they face those challenges?
- Do you like to do crafts? What do you like to make? What sorts of things can you make that could help someone else?
- Do you and a friend or family member care about the same things? How could you start a project with them to do something for what you care about?

ALEXANDRA SKINNER (2013)

"It just takes one person to start something and it will just keep growing from there."

Project: After School Art Program

- Established in 2011
- Raised $4,500 in money and art supplies
- Developed lesson plans for students
- Served over 250 students
- Developed a website that provides 36 weeks of project plans

When school budgets are cut, among the first things to be reduced or eliminated are art and music classes. This happens despite the fact that numerous national studies have shown that kids who take art and music classes develop language, motor, problem-solving, and decision-making skills more easily. They also tend to do better in a variety of subject areas ranging from math and science to social studies and language arts.

Exposure to the arts advances our country's culture, technology, and health. If more students are exposed to art and music, more of them not only will become artists and musicians but also administrators of arts organizations and arts supporters and advocates, which will lead to a more vibrant society. If more students do well in mathematics, more of them will become engineers and architects, which will lead to more inventions, safer buildings and bridges, and better solutions for technological problems. If more students do well in science, more of them become doctors and researchers, which will lead to better healthcare, disease prevention and treatment, and improved physical and mental health for us all.

When Lincoln High School freshman Ali Skinner noticed that art programming in Vincennes, Indiana, schools was being cut—and that after-school care was not a productive or an educational time for students—she created the After School Art

Program (ASAP) with the intention of addressing both problems.

Ali started the program by going into the elementary schools in Vincennes once a week. She spent between 60 and 90 minutes doing art projects with students. Those sessions allowed them to develop creativity, express themselves, and feel a sense of pride in completing their projects.

Ali with some of the many art supplies she has donate to her After School Art Progran

Ali and the teachers she worked with saw something special happen with the students. The program made them engaged and productive. They embraced the opportunity that ASAP gave them to explore new techniques and develop new skills. Ali also watched students with autism, Down syndrome, or other obstacles in their daily lives thrive when given the chance to create art.

From the beginning, ASAP caught on. Ali wrote grants to pay for supplies and coordinated volunteers to help her. She also trademarked the ASAP name and logo to ensure she retained control over the program's future. By 2014 it had expanded to all of the school corporations in Vincennes and surrounding Vigo County, as well as to schools in four other states.

The Power of Children Award provided more exposure for ASAP, which Ali used to help raise awareness of the program even further.

Ali created 36 weeks of lessons for students, including projects like this fish bowl.

She developed a website that provided lesson plans for art projects, volunteer manuals, and fund-raising ideas so schools could implement ASAP on their own. Her long-range goal for the program, which she was still running as a Lincoln High junior in 2014, was to take ASAP to schools nationwide.

QUESTIONS TO THINK ABOUT
- When people talk about "the arts," what do they mean? What kinds of art are there?
- How do you think that making art or playing music affects a person's ability to learn or do other things?
- Do you like to look at art? What do you think about when you are looking at it?
- How do you express yourself creatively? How did you learn to do this?
- Have you ever thought about being an artist of some kind when you grow up? What types of careers are available?

MAKENZIE SMITH (2013)

*"It doesn't matter how small your organization or activity may be.
You're still making a difference in the world by just helping one person."*

Project: Makenzie's Coat Closet
- Established in 2007
- Collected 19,000 total coats
- Used 97% of funds raised to purchase new coats, hats, gloves, and scarves
- Raised $8,000 in 2014
- Helped 20 agencies annually

Makenzie was only 7 years old when she decided to find a way to help others.

In 2007, Makenzie Smith and her classmates sat with their 2nd-grade teacher, who told them about the less fortunate people in the world. Makenzie's teacher also talked about how cold the winter was supposed to be that year. She told them that many people did not have the simple necessities in life, like a warm coat or a pair of gloves.

Although Makenzie was only 7 years old at the time, she asked herself, "What can I do to help?" That very day, she went home from school and told her parents that she wanted to start a coat collection for the homeless to keep them warm for the winter.

That was the start of Makenzie's Coat Closet. Determined to provide as many coats as possible, Makenzie asked friends and family members to give her any coats they didn't wear anymore. Once she had all of her donations in hand, she took them to an organization that could distribute them to the homeless.

But she didn't stop there. She did the same thing the next year and the next and the next. Each year Makenzie reached out to more and more people. She asked friends of friends and extended family for coats. She set up collection boxes at businesses, churches, and schools. As she reached out to more people, the word of what she was doing spread.

By the time Makenzie was a freshman at Borden Junior-Senior High School in Borden, Indiana, in 2014, she had her organization running smoothly. Each year she worked with local businesses and organizations to collect donations.

She set up contests to encourage students at schools and employees at businesses to donate coats. She ran a distribution day where all the coats, hats, scarves, and gloves were organized and local organizations came in to choose what they needed for the people they served. As she prepared for each coat drive season, Makenzie operated the Coat Closet's

During a busy distribution day, Makenzie pauses for a quick photo with some of the 19,000 coats she has collected.

Facebook and Twitter accounts and made sure to let those who donated know how much she appreciated it by writing thank-you letters.

Winning the Power of Children Award helped Makenzie expand her organization to agencies and shelters in Indiana and Kentucky, while publicity about the award highlighted Makenzie's Coat Closet's longstanding devotion to helping people in need. As a result, Makenzie received even more grants to purchase new coats. That helped meet one of the challenges she faced since starting the coat drives—having coats for small children and infants.

Makenzie said her real reward, though, was handing over a new coat or winter wear to someone who needed it. "It's really overwhelming to know that something so simple can make someone so happy," she said.

QUESTIONS TO THINK ABOUT
- Do you think you have too few, too many, or just enough coats and winter clothes? What makes you think that?
- Have you ever donated clothing to someone? How do you think that helped someone else?
- How would you feel if you were in the cold without a coat and no one to help you?
- Do you or other members of your family have coats, gloves, or scarves you don't need or want any more? Is there a shelter or other community organization where you could donate those items?

MY'KAH KNOWLIN (2014)

"Find something you're passionate about and start looking for how you can bring about a positive change."

Project: Boxes of Love

- Established in 2011
- Raised $75,000
- Sent 3,000 care packages of toys, snacks, and hygiene items

My'Kah is an honor roll student who finds the time to help disaster victims

One of the deadliest tornadoes in history struck Joplin, Missouri, on May 22, 2011. It was a powerful multiple vortex tornado that was rated an EF5, the highest rating on a tornado measurement scale. Wind speeds in excess of 200 miles per hour resulted in the deaths of more than 150 people and $2.8 billion in property damage.

Three hundred miles away in Lincoln, Nebraska, 10-year-old My'Kah Knowlin heard about the tragedy and immediately wanted to help the children of Joplin.

My'Kah brainstormed with her mother about what she could do. She knew she could not fix everything for the storm's victims. However, she also knew that having some basic things could be the first step back to a normal life.

She decided that the best way to help would be to gather up shoe boxes and stuff them full of toys, snacks, and hygiene items. My'Kah set a modest goal of creating 100 boxes to give away. To get materials for what she would eventually call Boxes of Love, My'Kah asked family, friends, and businesses in Lincoln for donations. She spoke on local radio stations and met with reporters to spread the word. She also asked her school for help and held garage sales to raise money.

Because of My'Kah's efforts, 3,000 children received care packages, many more than her initial goal. Those care packages brought smiles to faces that had gone too long without them. The boxes helped thousands have something to hold onto and call their own.

So many people got involved with her project that she was also able to help residents of Moore, Oklahoma, when it was also hit by a tornado in 2013. When a moving truck did not show to take supplies to Moore, she lined up volunteers to drive their cars nearly seven hours from Lincoln to deliver the supplies.

As an 8th-grader at Lux Middle School in Lincoln in 2014, My'Kah was a member of the Student Council, the Smart Girls Club, and the Anti-Bullying Club (which she founded), as well as the volleyball and cheering teams. An honor roll student, My'Kah hoped eventually to travel around the country speaking about the importance of community service.

My'Kah's passion for helping others extended beyond Boxes of Love. In 2014 high school was still in the future, she said she wanted to go to college one day to become an obstetrician specializing in high-risk pregnancies. She also dreamed of expanding Boxes of Love and turning it into a nonprofit organization that would continue to help children facing loss and disaster.

Three years into her project, My'Kah said she had been surprised by how many emotions her work evoked. "I had a mother come up to me crying," she recalled, "because her child was running with bubbles from his box and laughing. It was the first time she had seen him smile in the three months since the disaster. I knew then that what I was doing was making a difference and changing lives."

Although she was 300 miles away when a deadly tornado struck Joplin, Missouri, My'Kay knew she had to help.

QUESTIONS TO THINK ABOUT

- What things do you own that are very important to you? How would you feel if you lost them?
- My'Kah used shoeboxes to deliver care packages to others. How could you reuse materials for a service project?
- Have you (or has someone you know) lived through a natural disaster? If so, what happened? How did you (or they) feel? How did you (or they) deal with those feelings? How could someone who has lived through a natural disaster use the experience to help others?

ISAAC MCFARLAND (2014)

"Never give up on your dreams no matter what obstacles you may run up upon."

Project: Game Changers Tackling Hunger

- Established in 2011
- Raised $25,000 through donations and awards
- Collected 12,000 pounds of food
- Donated 1,500 boxes and 1,000 bags of food
- Benefited 2,000 children
- Trained 26 youth ambassadors to educate their peers about healthy lifestyles

The biggest difference between a philanthropist and someone who isn't one is not how much money the philanthropist donates, how many hours he or she volunteers, or even how many people his or her efforts help. The biggest difference is that a

Isaac packing supplies in his ongoing fight against hunger.

philanthropist does *something* to help out somebody else. That is the reason that Power of Children Award winners like Isaac McFarland stand out.

Isaac was a student at Caddo Parish Magnet High School in Shreveport, Louisiana, one of the top schools in the state, when he came face-to-face with childhood hunger. The school is located in a neighborhood

Isaac continues to effect change w his Tackle Box progr

where many residents live in poverty, while Caddo's students, many of whom live elsewhere, do not.

As a freshman, Isaac saw children from the neighborhood walking to other schools. He volunteered at the local recreation center to tutor some of them, which allowed him to get to know them and the problems they faced. One of the most serious problems was access to good food.

After seeing that the neighborhood's food bank was overwhelmed by people in need, Isaac created Game Changers Tackling Hunger, with the goal of eliminating hunger in the community. He started small by donating beef grown on his family's cattle farm, using meat from his 4-H steer. He then asked friends, classmates, officials, and junior cattlemen to donate food items or create what Isaac called "Tackle Boxes." After that, Isaac started food drives.

The Tackle Boxes (and later "Tackle Bags") were filled with healthy, non-perishable food items. Game Changers gave those Tackles Boxes to children in homes where food was scarce. Isaac's project was supported so strongly that he expanded his goal to ending hunger not only in his school's community but also in communities across the nation. Ultimately, he said, he wanted to see hunger totally eliminated worldwide.

Isaac also ran a youth ambassador program that selected students from elementary, middle, and high schools to educate their peers about healthy living. As of 2014, the program had helped 12,000 young people learn more about food and healthy lifestyles.

Occasionally Isaac ran into someone who didn't think food drives were important. His reply, he said, was this: "Food drives are not important because you are not hungry, but if you are one of the individuals that did not know where your next meal is coming from, then this food drive would be very important to you!"

Isaac's dedication to ending hunger led to even more health-related opportunities. He was selected to be part of a national youth board that focuses on eliminating obesity. That opportunity allowed him to travel the country and meet others with projects like his. He also spoke on an anti-smoking panel after being invited by a former U.S. Surgeon General. Isaac even travelled to a large farm to learn about farming techniques that get the freshest vegetables to children living in food deserts (urban neighborhoods without grocery stores or other access to healthy food).

Winning the Power of Children Award enabled Isaac and Game Changers Tackling Hunger to continue the fight against hunger. The grant that came with the award allowed him to continue the Tackle Box program, as well as to expand his ambassador program.

When Isaac wasn't working to end hunger, he used his free time to work on his family's cattle ranch

Isaac posing with his award leaf in November 2014.

and participate in 4-H. He was also active in his school's orchestra and was named to the Louisiana All-State Orchestra. After high school, he planned on going to college and majoring in accounting or a health field.

Recipient of many honors for his efforts, including the National Points of Light Award and the Louisiana Blue Cross Blue Shield Angel Award, Isaac was determined not to abandon what he started with Game Changers Tackling Hunger. "Because we live in a society of plenty, we do not think hunger is as prevalent in our communities," he said. "I have learned that when people are faced with the staggering numbers associated with hunger they are more than willing to help. It is my job to keep those statistics on hunger before the American public, so that we can end hunger."

QUESTIONS TO THINK ABOUT

- What is something that you have done for someone else? Why did you decide to do it?
- Have you ever helped someone you did not know? Why or why not?
- Have your parents or guardians ever said that you could not have something at the grocery store? Why do you think they said no? How did it make you feel?
- Do you have a healthy lifestyle? How do you know? What types of food do you eat and what activities do you do?
- How does eliminating hunger help society as well as individuals?

TATUM PARKER (2014)

"Be passionate about life and all that it offers."

Project: Tatum's Bags of Fun

- Established in 2008
- Donated 1,800 care packages filled with toys and games

Tatum Parker knows what it is like to be a kid stuck in the hospital. The Indianapolis, Indiana native battled cancer twice and came out a winner both times. However, the treatment that she received left her, like many other young patients, feeling weak.

While recovering from her treatments Tatum was bored. Even though her parents and family visited her, which helped her cope with the boredom of lying in bed, Tatum knew that not everyone was as lucky. Sometimes children who are sick don't have family or friends who can visit them as frequently as they would like. Tatum wanted to make sure they had something to do.

She developed a project called Tatum's Bags of Fun. Her goal was to give a bag to every child diagnosed with cancer in Indiana. The bags include about $350 worth of age-appropriate games, toys, and activities ranging from Leapsters, iPods, and Nintendo DS units to books, crafts, and movies.

Tatum's bags brought smiles to almost 2,000 children in Indiana at Riley Hospital for Children.

Tatum maintained that age should have nothing to do with what a person can accomplish.

Even though she suffered a cancer relapse herself, Tatum helped bring smiles to nearly 2,000 children at Riley Hospital for Children and Peyton Manning Children's Hospital, both in Indianapolis; IU Health North in Carmel, Indiana; Memorial Hospital of South Bend, Indiana; and Proton Beam Therapy Center in Bloomington, Indiana.

Tatum also developed a Kids' Board that helped her with fund-raising, project management, and delivery of the bags. The teenagers that made up the Kids' Board not only helped expand Tatum's project, but also learned how to develop their own community service projects.

Since she had spent so much time with doctors and nurses as both a patient and a philanthropist, Tatum became interested in the medical field. Though only an 8th-grader at Westlane Middle School in Indianapolis in 2014, she knew she wanted to work in a field that involved helping others.

Tatum's Bags of Fun was featured on *NBC Nightly News with Brian Williams*, and Indiana University men's basketball coach Tom Crean chose the organization as his charity of choice for the Infiniti Coaches Charity Challenge. But Tatum didn't let the attention interfere with her quest for new and interesting ways to raise money for cancer research and have a positive impact on children with cancer. She started a triathlon team and also began an annual "shave-a-thon" to raise money.

The winner of several awards for her service work, Tatum maintained that age should have nothing to do with what a person can accomplish. "Children should realize that they can do anything they put their minds to. They have the same opportunities and abilities to make an impact as adults do."

QUESTIONS TO THINK ABOUT

- Have you ever been too sick to do something that you wanted to do? How did that experience make you feel? What activities could you have done while you were sick to make you feel better?
- Not all cancer is the same and not everyone will have the same side effects if they are sick. Why do the kinds of things that Tatum included in her Bags of Fun help make even the sickest patients feel better?
- What careers are interesting to you? What service projects could you start today that are connected to your dream career?

MARIAH REYNOLDS (2014)

"Every good deed is important and every hour of service is precious."

Project: gLOVE One Another

- Established in 2008
- Donated 2,000 backpacks
- Sent 110,000 letters to soldiers
- Involved 4,500 volunteers

Malcolm Gladwell, a writer who examined what it takes to be successful in the book *Outliers*, wrote that the key to being really good at something is practicing it for 10,000 hours. That would be like working a job for eight hours a day for three and a half years.

By 2014 Mariah, an 8th-grader at the School for Creative and Performing Arts in Cincinnati, Ohio, was well on her way to the 10,000-hour mark, having spent nearly 6,000 hours with her organization gLOVE One Another. The organization donated warm clothing and backpacks filled with books and school supplies to children and schools that had lost everything in natural disasters such as Hurricane Sandy in 2012 and the Moore, Oklahoma, tornado and Boulder, Colorado, flood in 2013.

Mariah used part of her $2,000 POC grant to create small scholarshi for children of active duty milita personn

Having a good idea like gLOVE One Another is much easier than making it a reality, however. To provide the help that the victims of natural disasters need required money, so when Mariah discovered that raising it was hard, she got creative. In addition to having garage sales and collection drives, she also started "backwards yard sales."

She would go to yard sales in and around her hometown of Moores Hill, Indiana, and collect unsold items. The sellers were happy to get rid of stuff they no longer wanted or could not sell, and Mariah then sold the items at a fund-raising event for her organization. Anything not sold was either donated or, with materials like used denim, recycled to create insulation for housing.

Mariah provided holiday cheer with many activities.

Many of the Power of Children Award winners, like Mariah Reynolds, begin the process by working diligently on projects they care about for 10 to 15 hours a week. Because of this consistent commitment, they become good at running organizations and helping others.

Mariah's organization helped more than 15,000 people. In addition to helping disaster victims, she also mounted an ambitious letter-writing campaign to send 100,000 thank-you and Valentine's Day cards and letters to U.S. military veterans and active duty soldiers. She surpassed her goal by almost 10,000 cards and letters.

Teens involved with her project learned the value (to them and others) of community service. Because the world is a global community, Mariah believed it was important for everyone to take care of one another.

Mariah planned to use the $2,000 grant that came with her Power of Children Award to create a small scholarship for children of active duty military personnel as well as to purchase items for her organization and upgrade its website.

While most of her free time was taken up with gLOVE One Another, Mariah also was active in 4-H, the National Honor Society, and an anti-bullying club. Despite sometimes feeling tired and a bit defeated by the demands of running her organization, Mariah said she had learned that those moments always passed, leaving her inspired again and ready to go on.

"I discovered how much volunteer service can change you," she said. "It creates confidence, leadership, and ambition."

QUESTIONS TO THINK ABOUT

- How could you help adults explain natural disasters to young children? Write a list or do some research.
- What is something that you are particularly good at? How long did it take you to get good at it? What did you do to get better?
- What do others mean when they say that we have a "global economy" or live in a "global community"?
- How would you raise money for an organization you believe in? What is your most creative idea?
- Do you participate in any extracurricular activities? What are they? How can you apply what you learn in your extracurricular activities to philanthropy in the real world?

KENDRA SPRINGS (2014)

"You can't make an impact if you never try."

Project: Kendra's Call for Komfort

- Established in 2011
- Raised $50,000
- Provided 150 care packages to hospitalized children
- Gave restaurant and gas gift cards to hospital staff
- Donated money to the art therapy program and the Stem Cell Unit at Riley Hospital for Children

Kendra was in the eighth grade when she won her Power of Children Award

When Kendra Springs was being treated for neuroblastoma, a type of childhood cancer, she was discouraged by the lack of things she could do and the lack of comfortable clothing she had to wear. She was stuck in bed, in a hospital gown, with nothing to do. Worse yet, she saw other children going through the same thing.

As a young girl with interest in fashion and community service, Kendra created Kendra's Call for Komfort, an organization that provided new clothing, activities, and gift cards to children who have been hospitalized. Kendra formed the organization mere months after her cancer diagnosis. She helped raise funds and plan events throughout her own treatments.

Kendra spent at least five hours each week working on behalf of her organization. She planned four annual fundraisers. Her determination to help others inspired her entire community to show their support with fund-raising or volunteering. Students at Plainfield High School in Plainfield, Indiana, started a student board that raised money for Kendra's Call for Komfort. The varsity kicker on the football team also raised money through local businesses, convincing them to donate money for every field goal and extra point the team made. Those promises alone raised over $13,000 for Kendra's project.

The funds went towards what Kendra calls "comfy care packages." Staff members at Riley Hospital for Children in Indianapolis, its north campus in Carmel, Indiana, and Peyton Manning Children's Hospital in Indianapolis helped identify children who might appreciate the bags. Kendra, who enjoyed shopping almost as much as she enjoyed helping others, spent about $250 on such items as pajamas and other comfortable clothes, gift cards, and games. Each bag was personalized to meet the needs of a specific child.

Kendra was also able to donate money to various hospital units and programs that either provided treatments or helped children feel better during their treatments. She even donated six medical play carts and two toy medical exam machines. Children could play with these machines to help them feel less anxious if they had to be examined by the real machines.

Although only an eighth grader at Saint Susanna Middle School in Plainfield, Indiana, in the 2014–2015 school year, Kendra already had her sights set high. Winner of her school's Mother Teresa Award and a National Junior Honors Society member, she hoped to expand Kendra's Call for Komfort nationwide, while someday working in the arts or fashion design.

The Power of Children Award four-year scholarship reduced the amount of money she had to save for college, meaning she would have more money to give to her organization. "Generosity," said Kendra, "creates positive change."

Kendra enlisted help from nurses to distribute her 150 care packages.

QUESTIONS TO THINK ABOUT

- Have you ever designed your own clothes or donated clothes you have made? If you wanted to learn how to do this, where could you find more information?
- Have you ever had to have a medical test or surgery done that made you uncomfortable or scared? What did others do for you to help you feel more comfortable?
- There are other things besides cancer that can make a person sick. What are some other diseases or illnesses that nonprofit organizations raise funds for?
- What is your favorite subject in school? What is your favorite activity just for fun? How could you combine those two favorite things into a volunteer project?

10 TIPS FOR MAKING A DIFFERENCE

1. **Define what is needed.** In the stories you have read, all the Power of Children Award winners addressed a need. Soldiers and veterans needed supplies. People who were unemployed needed jobs. Those who were poor needed food, education, or clothing. The winners asked themselves one question: What do other people need? Before they could help solve problems, they had to know who needed what.

   If you want to make an impact in your community (or anywhere else in the world), start by finding out what is missing from other peoples' lives. Watch the news and read newspapers, online articles, and books, and go out and build relationships with people in your community.

2. **Choose a cause that you are passionate about.** What do you care about? What motivates you? What problem would you like to solve? If you are excited about what you are doing, then it will show and the work will not seem as difficult. If you pick something you are passionate about, your desire to create change and make a difference will inspire others to action and keep you motivated and engaged in your project for a long time.

3. **Learn what others are doing and offer to help.** A lot of the Power of Children Award winners started their own organizations. That can be hard work. First look around to see if there is already an organization that's dealing with the topic or cause that interests you. If there is, perhaps you can find a way to work together, either as a volunteer in the organization or by developing a project that's an extension of what the organization is doing.

   Volunteer at a service organization. You will gain experience helping people while you learn how organizations operate. You may also learn that the cause you're interested in is more complex than you realized. Not only will you have the chance to work with other people who are passionate about making a difference, you will gain the experience you will need to lead an organization in the future.

4. **Believe in yourself and ask for help.** Sometimes doing the right thing is not popular. Your friends or family members may think your efforts are a waste of time. It will be up to you to decide how you are going to handle such difficulties. Perhaps you will challenge them to join you. Maybe you will invite them to a social event where they can get involved with your cause and have fun at the same time.

The most important thing to remember is this: If you have picked a noble cause you are passionate about, it won't matter what others think. Your reward will be knowing that you have had a positive impact on the lives of others.

Don't forget that many people and companies want to help you help others. Various organizations and businesses give out awards and grants to those who are actively involved in community service projects. Once you start your own organization or begin volunteering at an existing one, start applying for grants and awards. The Power of Children Awards are a great example!

You may be shy or nervous or not have many resources to use. Do not be afraid to speak up and reach out to people. Your enthusiasm for your project will inspire others. And remember, if you help only one person, you have already changed the world for the better.

5. **Understand the power of one.** One question you may ask yourself if the problem you want to tackle seems too big: How can one person possibly make a difference? The answer is: By trying. Whatever the problem is that you want to solve, it didn't develop overnight. Neither will its solution. Be patient. Take one step at a time.

Many people around you will tell you no one can change anything. That's because changing the way things are is hard work, much harder than not doing anything. Sometimes the older people get, the more they think that things cannot or will not change.

A lot of Power of Children Award winners faced obstacles because adults often considered them too young to do anything meaningful. But the young people persevered and made big impacts on communities around the world. In the process they often inspired those same adults to be more charitable.

6. **Start small.** Start with your community, your family, your school, your church, or maybe just one person. Carry groceries in for a neighbor, rake leaves in your neighborhood, or give some of your allowance to charity. Imagine if everyone worked to change just one person's life! Look back through the Power of Children Award winners, too. Many of them got started by simply doing something nice for one person or a small group of people.

7. **Now think big, and then think bigger.** Although you start small, you can still dream big. Take a sheet of paper and write down a passion or a goal. Some people call this a vision statement, and some others call this the "big picture." You can also make a list. List all the things you would do if you had unlimited resources. Let all your ideas out. Only after this should you evaluate them. You may find a way to make something work with the resources you have that you used to think was impossible.

8. **Keep going.** The projects in this book are impressive because the winners kept going. They helped one person, then two, then 10. In many cases it became hundreds of people, even thousands. Helping people can be a lot like exercising or learning something new. If you keep at something for long enough, it begins adding up. If you helped a different person each day for a year, that would be 365 people. Set attainable goals, and you will be surprised how fast a project can grow.

Keep a list of your accomplishments in a folder on your computer. Save letters, notes from others, poems, positive phrases, or other things that make you feel good, too. You can always look back at these and what you have done in the past to understand how far you have come, and you can remind yourself that you are making a difference.

9. **Surround yourself with people who will help you achieve your goals.** They should be people who can encourage you when you become discouraged. They should be people who believe in you and your cause. They should be people who will help you stick to the promises you make to yourself and others.

   You will have to set priorities. If you have a team around you that will help you organize your priorities, you will be even more successful.

   This is important because you will face obstacles. There will be setbacks. Having a strong team surrounding you helps you feel strong when you hit roadblocks, face people who do not believe in your cause, or struggle to stay passionate about what you are doing.

10. **Enjoy the moment.** It can be easy to get caught up in helping others, planning events, and meeting your goals. Be sure to take a step back every once in a while and appreciate the impact you have made. Congratulate yourself for a job well done, and enjoy the work that you do for others. When you're tired from working hard, taking time to recognize your own efforts can help reinvigorate you, too.

ORGANIZATIONS AND RESOURCES

This section includes website addresses for organizations that you can become a part of today. Many are featured in this book and are still actively creating a positive impact. Other organizations are also included, especially those that have many locations across the United States. Of course, you are always encouraged to volunteer with *any* credible local organization that helps others!

While these organizations are divided up into categories, it does not mean that these categories are the only ones that the Power of Children Awards recognize. The Children's Museum of Indianapolis is always looking for unique, engaging, and inspiring projects that benefit others. If you are interested in applying for the Power of Children Awards, visit The Children's Museum of Indianapolis website at childrensmuseum.org.

Building a Global Community and Impact

Hola Bloomington
POCA Winner: Abraxas Segundo García
http://bloomington.in.gov/hola

Ken-ya Help Us?
POCA Winner: Nate Osborne
http://www.globalinterfaithpartnership.org/umoja/educationalsupport/kenya-carnival/

Kids Change the World
POCA Winner: Christopher Yao
http://www.kidschangetheworld.org/

Kiva
http://www.kiva.org/

Peace Corps
http://www.peacecorps.gov/volunteer/learn/

United Nations Volunteers
http://www.unv.org/how-to-volunteer.html

Domestic Violence

National Coalition Against Domestic Violence
http://www.ncadv.org/

The National Domestic Violence Hotline
http://www.thehotline.org/

Sheltering Wings
POCA Winner: Shelby Mitchell
http://www.shelteringwings.org

Education and Literacy

After School Art Program (ASAP)
POCA Winner: Ali Skinner
http://www.afterschoolartprogram.org/

American Library Association
http://www.ala.org/

Association of Bookmobile & Outreach Services
http://abos-outreach.org/

Educate Jamaica
POCA Winner: Jill Osterhus
http://educatejamaica.weebly.com/index.html

Find a Book a Home Foundation/ History Makers of the Future
POCA Winner: Carah Austin
http://www.findabookahome.com/

Little Free Library
http://littlefreelibrary.org/

Net Literacy
POCA Winner: Daniel Kent
http://www.netliteracy.org/

Read Indeed
POCA Winner: Maria Keller
http://www.readindeed.org/

Watts Backpack Baggers
POCA Winner: Kaylin Fanta
http://www.wattsbackpackbaggers.com/home.html

Environment and Healthy Living

Greening Forward
POCA Winner: Charles Orgbon III
http://greeningforward.org/

SMART2bfit
POCA Winner: Madeline Cumbey
http://www.smart2bfit.org/

World Wildlife Fund
http://wwf.panda.org/how_you_can_help/volunteer/

Kids Helping Kids & Community Empowerment

Empower Orphans
POCA Winner: Neha Gupta
http://www.empowerorphans.org/

gLOVE One Another
POCA Winner: Mariah Reynolds
http://www.gloveoneanother.org/

KI EcoCenter
POCA Winner: Nicholas Clifford
http://kiecocenterorg.ipage.com/demo22/

Olivia's Cause
POCA Winner: Olivia Rusk
http://oliviascause.vpweb.com/Home.html

PCs for Youth
POCA Winner: Kyle Gough
http://pcsforyouth.org/

United Way of America
http://www.unitedway.org/take-action/volunteer/

Youth Embracing Service (YES)
POCA Winners: Amanda and Grant Mansard
http://youthembracingservice.org/

Mental Health Awareness

Mental Health America of Greater Indianapolis
POCA Winner: Sarah Wood
http://www.mhaindy.net/

Suicide Prevention Hotline
http://www.suicidepreventionlifeline.org/getinvolved/volunteer.aspx

Natural Disaster Aid

American Red Cross
http://www.redcross.org/support/volunteer/opportunities#step1

Boxes of Love
POCA Winner: My'Kah Knowlin
http://boxesoflove.net/

Project K.I.D.
POCA Winner: Jacob Baldwin
www.project-kid.org

We Care Act
POCA Winner: Grace Li
http://wecareact.org/

Physical Health Awareness and Support

Freedom Chairs of Indiana
POCA Winner: Tim Balz
http://freedomchairs.org/

Hats of Hope
POCA Winner: Kaylee Shirrell
https://sites.google.com/site/hatsofhopeinfo/

Keegan's Clan/St. Baldrick's
POCA Winner: Keegan McCarthy
http://www.stbaldricks.org/

Kendra's Call for Komfort
POCA Winner: Kendra Springs
http://kendrascallforkomfort.org/

Little Wish Foundation
POCA Winner: Liz Niemiec
http://littlewishfoundation.org/

Livestrong Foundation
http://www.livestrong.org/Take-Action

Nana's Cancer Miracles
POCA Winner: Ashley Slayton
http://nanascancermiracles.com/

Tatum's Bags of Fun
POCA Winner: Tatum Parker
http://tatums.bagsoffun.org/

YMCA
http://www.ymca.net/volunteer/

Poverty and Hunger

Feeding America
http://feedingamerica.org/get-involved/volunteer.aspx

Free Rice
http://www.freerice.com

Makenzie's Coat Closet
POCA Winner: Makenzie Smith
http://makenziescoatcloset.com/

Support for the Homeless

The Coalition for Homelessness Intervention and Prevention in Indianapolis (CHIP Indy)
http://www.chipindy.org/how-to-help/volunteer/

Horizon House
http://www.horizonhouse.cc/

National Coalition for the Homeless
http://www.nationalhomeless.org/want_to_help/

Volunteers of America
http://www.voa.org/Get-Help/National-Network-of-Services/Homelessness

Support for Soldiers

The American Legion
http://www.legion.org/troops

Operation U.S. Troop Support
POCA Winner: Alison Mansfield
http://operationustroopsupport.org/

United Service Organizations (USO)
http://www.uso.org/ways-to-volunteer.aspx

VETSupport
POCA Winner: Krystal Shirrell
Website: https://sites.google.com/site/hatsofhopeinfo/

Veterans of Foreign Wars (VFW)
http://www.vfw.org/CommunityService/

U.S. Department of Veterans Affairs
http://www.volunteer.va.gov/apps/VolunteerNow/

How to Start and Run an Organization

Foundation Center
http://www.foundationcenter.org/

Grant Space
http://grantspace.org

The Seattle Foundation's Resources for Youth and Family Philanthropy
http://www.seattlefoundation.org

Small Business Administration
http://www.sba.gov

Society for Nonprofits
http://www.snpo.org

Wikihow's How to Start a 501(c)(3) Nonprofit Organization
http://www.wikihow.com/Start-a-501c3-Nonprofit-Organization

Youth and Philanthropy Initiative
http://www.goypi.org/ypi-resources/for-students.html

Other Organizations & Resources

Do Something
https://www.dosomething.org/

GenerationOn
http://www.generationon.org/service-clubs/join/about

Habitat for Humanity
http://www.habitat.org/local

The Humane Society
http://www.humanesociety.org/

These Kids Mean Busines$
http://www.thesekidsmeanbusiness.org/

United We Serve
http://www.serve.gov

Youth Changing the World
http://www.ysa.org/

ABOUT THE AUTHORS

Skip Berry is an Indianapolis-based freelance writer who frequently works on projects for The Children's Museum, including serving as the chief writer for the museum's online history. A former feature writer for the *Indianapolis Star*, he is the author or co-author of several books about local cultural institutions, as well as young adult biographies of E.E. Cummings, Emily Dickinson, Langston Hughes, Gordon Parks, and William Carlos Williams. An experienced screenwriter, he has written a variety of feature film and television series scripts that have won numerous awards. He is the head writer and co-producer of a multimedia project on the history of jazz in Indianapolis, which will begin production in 2016.

Andrew Kimmel is an English instructor and freelance editor. He was named Bepko Scholar & University Fellow at Indiana University Purdue University Indianapolis, where he earned master's degrees in English and philosophy. Andrew has previously written online content for The Honor Society of Nursing, Sigma Theta Tau International and The Children's Museum of Indianapolis, Inc. He was recognized by Indiana INTERNnet as Intern of the Year for his internship project, *The Power of Children: Ordinary Youth Making Extraordinary Differences*. Andrew lives in Indianapolis with his partner, Mandi, and two cats.

Printed in the United States
By Bookmasters